Run Softly, Go Fast

Barbara Wersba

Atheneum *1973* New York

Run Softly, Go Fast

H E'S DEAD, but I can't feel anything. Not now after the funeral. Not a month ago when he sat up in the hospital bed, high on morphine and stringing paper clips together. I kept wondering where he'd got the paper clips. There was a box of them on the table and he was stringing them together like a child. Perfect irony: stoned on morphine and outraged by all the "bums and hippies" who smoke pot. He cried for morphine at the end—I was in the corridor but I heard it. So did Mom and Uncle Ben. Ben was praying, his face pale and humble, and I hated him for that. Please God, do this. Do that God, please. God, save my brother. . . . Prayers are words, and words change nothing. He's buried in Brooklyn—the stubborn face, the thick fingers stained by cigars, the short legs. I wonder why he looked so different when I was a kid. . . . I feel numb tonight, disconnected. The loft is filled with shadows and the portrait I'm doing of Maggie looks weird in the dusk. Mom thought I'd come back to Riverside Drive now and live in my old room, just like nothing had happened. Why can't she and Ben see the games they play? Ben's an esthete, a scholar, but he plays games. Only his aren't money and security and possessions. The riches he hoards are spiritual. Can't they see that you can't hoard *anything?* We get born and we die with only one possession: ourselves.

The funeral was such a farce. That rabbi didn't even know Dad. Just hired for the occasion like an entertainer. Which is what all the priests and rabbis are—entertainers telling stale jokes. The place was impersonal, a few dozen chairs and a lectern. Flowers were withering in the heat. And the minute we went out to the limousine they started getting ready for the next funeral: death on the assembly line. Why did he seem so different when I was little? I looked at him in that hospital bed, high on morphine and babbling about the office, the business, and I had a sudden memory of being five. The bungalow in the Catskills . . . I don't want to think about it. He said I was a bum to let a girl support me. As if painting wasn't work. Bums and hippies, hippies and bums—you could make a song out of it. "At least get engaged," he kept saying. "Did I raise you for this? To live like a degenerate in the East Village? What kind of family does a girl come from that she should live openly with a young man, not even being engaged?" He was so crude—even when he bought Shulman out of the business and started wearing $300.00 suits. Even when he got the place in Florida and hired a butler for parties. I used to shudder at those attempts at "class." But the summers in the Catskills. . . .

I wish Maggie would come home. I want to make love. Which would shock Ben—right after a funeral. But sex is life and tonight I want life very much. My life, not his. My thoughts, my speech, my hands that can paint. If he'd had his way I would be starting my third year of college . . . so incredible. Then graduate and enter the business. Then marry and drink too much and watch TV. And fill my existence with *things* to make up for the grief of it. He always had his car polished once a month, which is why I never drove it: one scratch and he would go to pieces. "What's the matter you can't be more careful? Six thousand dollars for a car and you drive like a maniac." He loved the car better than he loved any of us. Insane. People die and all that's left is a lot of junk. Gold cufflinks, TV sets, golf clubs. There weren't any real friends at the funeral except the Lowensteins. It's funny, but that was the only part that bothered me.

Be honest. He was a bastard and you hated him.

After the cemetery we went back to Riverside Drive for lunch—me, Mom, Ben and the Lowensteins—like we were celebrating something. Which maybe we were. Then they began talking about the old days: what a great guy Leo was, how much people admired him. It was like listening to a fairy tale. Ruth Lowenstein shook her head at me. "That long hair, Davy!" But she isn't so bad. At least

(5)

she came to the funeral. . . . My hair was long when I was little too. I was so pretty that people thought I was a girl—and he hated that. Masculinity was crucial to him, and if I remember anything about the Catskills it's those endless games of ball. Ben would be on the porch reading some book while Dad pitched to me in the yard. The funny thing is how different he seemed in those days.

Remember what you said to Rick a few years ago: "I won't be free till he's dead." So you've got your wish. Only it doesn't seem like he's dead—just down in Florida, lying by the pool. He loved telling people how much things cost, tried to impress the buyers that way, but none of them came to his funeral. Man, would that have hurt him—but he would never have shown it. "What can you expect from that class of people?" he would have said. "Ignoramuses. The business world is full of them. Believe me, for my friends I look elsewhere." (But Leo, you didn't have any friends. You cut everyone's throat.)

Why can't I write about those summers? I want to keep writing till Maggie comes home. I want to keep the darkness out. . . . What was the beach like? White pebbles. I used to put them in my mouth. And the lake went on forever, a black emerald. The air was so clear that you could hear people talking on the other side. Once I heard somebody over there say, "Harold, you really burn me up," and I thought the person was on fire. At night the moonlight looked like silver on the bureau, and I wanted to scoop it up and put it in a jar. But it would always vanish when I touched it. I told him about this and he said, "Such a dreamer I've got. *Shaifeleh,* don't you know you cannot touch the moon." I remembered that for a long time—the part about touching the moon. I must have been five that first summer. . . . The bungalow had a stale smell, but when the breeze came in it was like pine needles and milk. Maybe there were farms nearby. It's so clear suddenly. The path through the woods went down to the lake, and while I went wading Mom and Dad would spread out a blanket and play cards. They always had a portable radio going, but Ben would be reading as though he were on a desert island. I had a red boat. No, blue. And once when it drifted away I ran after it along the beach and found it by the Katz's dock. And then I saw . . . the Katz's two boys drowning a bird. "It's hurt," they said. "We're putting it out of its misery." But I knew it wasn't true. I knew that they liked drowning it and I cried.

Was it really like that, or am I making it up? No, it's like an old snapshot and I can see all of them: Ben in his rimless glasses, Mom in those denim shorts, Dad drinking beer out of the can. I can even see myself—too skinny, my eyes big and dark. I was frail, but it would have killed him to admit it. He saw me as an athlete and kept telling Ben what a good build I had. As though lies could make truth. But whenever anything bad happened, like the bird getting drowned, I would run to him and he would hold me. It's amazing how strong he seemed, how powerful. I liked the wiry hairs on his chest and the smell he had—of shaving lotion and cigars. And whenever he came to school I would be proud, because he seemed handsomer than anyone else's father. I drew pictures at school, but Mom was never in them. Just me and Dad, stick-figures with big heads. He kept all of them. I think the worst thing that happened was the day after he died, when Mom and I went through his things and found those pictures in the closet. . . . I'll keep writing till Maggie comes home and then I'll stop. I don't want any hangups about this. I want to let go. Which is what Rick used to tell me—let him go. But I couldn't, not even when I left home. I could never stop trying to prove myself, but no matter what I did it was wrong. I was always a bum, a failure, a hippie —his favorite word. He was so ignorant of life. A Jew who swallowed the Protestant Ethic and died of it.

That first summer at the lake . . . trees dappling the water, voices echoing on the other side. I would play in the shallow part for hours. The water was clear, but farther out it slipped into darkness, and I thought there was a monster sleeping on the bottom who could make the water calm or rough. Pine needles and milk, hot sun, Mom singing along with the radio. We would have lunch on the beach, and then we'd walk back to the bungalow where I'd take a nap with Mister Bear. Whenever I wet the bed I would say that he'd done it. Crimes—wetting the bed, going into their room without knocking, hiding in the closet. I couldn't have known much about God then, but I remember lying in that bed and praying to someone to make me good. Because to be good was to be loved. . . . (I went back to find the bird that day. And there it was on the Katz's beach, all limp and wet. I touched it and it felt horrible—one wing flopped out— but I didn't want to leave it there. So I took it to him. Is it dead? I asked. "No, *shaifeleh*. It's gone to heaven." And suddenly I saw that bird flying to heaven, where everything could live though it was dead, and I wanted to go too.)

Funny. The first time I took acid I hoped that I would see the truth about Dad—but the only truth I saw was that Marty Brooks was a snake. He'd been my friend for years, but when we took acid together he turned into a red snake with a black flickering tongue. And I realized that he was poisoning my life—which he was—and I wanted to kill him. But the second time . . . light fell through the air like colored glass, and I saw that there were colors within colors within colors. An endless spectrum that nobody else could see. A glass waterfall, jeweled and sparkling. The colors started to grow from my hands . . . So beautiful—showing me that art was inside me, not something to be reached for. It was flowing inside me like the glass waterfall. . . . Those games before dinner. I wanted so much to please him, but the harder I'd try the more I'd fail. Why couldn't he see that? He acted like it was the World Series or something, standing there slapping the mitt and yelling instructions. "Come on! You can do better than that. Keep your eye on the ball. Don't keep looking around, watch the ball. OK, OK, you pitch to me for a while. No, not underhand. You gotta swing your arm like this. See how easy?"

He kept slapping the mitt and grinning, waiting for me to turn into a ballplayer, a real little boy. ("He's a real boy, Ben. Look at that back, those shoulders.") So I was finished before I began—and on one of those occasions I started to whine for Mister Bear. He had been lost all day. "We'll find the teddy bear later," Leo said. "Come on! Pitch to me." I said that I wanted Mister Bear to pitch, and this really annoyed him. "What's the matter with you?" he asked. "Don't you like playing with Daddy?" And before I knew it, I had said no. All of a sudden he looked like he was going to weep. His face just crumpled up. Mom came out and took me back to the kitchen, but in that moment I wanted to die—because I loved him better than anyone and I had hurt his feelings. . . . Getting into his bed and playing that game with the flashlight under the covers. Riding on his shoulders in the water. Hiding his sunglasses . . . He was easygoing in those days, but not with Ben. "A whole college education, and this *meshuggener* works in a library. In the business world he could be making twenty thousand a year." Ben would always say the same thing —that he was happy—but that would only make Dad angrier. He loved business the way some people love God, and he could never stop criticizing Shulman. He didn't run the place right, the books were never in order, the salesmen were lazy. If it were *his* outfit he'd turn it into a gold mine. (And you did, Leo. In ten years you owned the firm. And a year after that you bought a place in Miami so you could entertain on a grand scale.)

How did I escape it? The little deaths of money and success. Rick. Before Rick, I was blind.

It was always the same after dinner. Dad would take the garbage out and settle down with Mom to listen to the radio. Ben would be reading by the window, holding his book up to the light. He seemed funny-looking in those days—the rimless glasses, the bushy hair—but when I grew older I saw that he had the face of a prophet, and I painted him. The bungalow had wicker furniture and faded rugs. Blue, I think. I would lie in the big armchair, listening to the wind in the pine trees and trying not to fall asleep. It was so peaceful with the radio playing low and

the wind outside, and Mom and Dad talking. Once . . .
when was it? That year or the next? I can't remember,
but once when I was dozing in the armchair a sound
woke me and I opened my eyes to see them kissing. Mom
said, "You shouldn't make love to me in front of him."
But he said, "Why not? You're my best girl, aren't you?"
They smiled at each other, and I suddenly knew something. As though I'd known it forever but just realized it.
And what I knew was that they were sleeping together.
This knowledge gave me a strange feeling, and as I
watched Mom the feeling got worse—because she was
looking at him in a very open way. I didn't want her to
look at him like that because he was *my* person, and his
bed was a place where we played games together. Then
all at once I realized why I couldn't go into their bedroom
without knocking, and fear came over me. . . . I don't
know what happened next. I think I ran to the couch and
got on his lap. But it was my first knowledge of sex. Not
learned. Known. Years later when he began playing
around I wondered why he'd married her—she was so
plain compared to the women he liked—but I know now.
She was part of the pattern he admired: Gentile, middle-
class, a year of college.

When I told Maggie that I hated my parents, she
said, "Never mind. We'll be each other's parents." And
we are. When I have nightmares she holds me like a child,
my face against her shoulder. She tells me stories, fairy
tales about giants and trolls and swans with silver wings,
waiting for the moment when I sink back into sleep, the
soft darkness. We are children together and lovers. Parents and friends. . . . I don't know if any of the things

(*11*)

I've written here are true. Memory lies, smooths over the rough parts. The things that hurt, like Rick, I can't talk about. Dad would never even meet Maggie, and the night I brought her home to supper was the night I knew he and I were finished. We really made an effort: Maggie in her green dress, me wearing a tie, a bottle of wine wrapped up as a gift. . . . The minute Mom opened the door I knew something was wrong. "Darling, you'll have to forgive Daddy but he's still at the office. Some sort of meeting." I knew it wasn't true but we went through the evening anyway, his place at the table empty. Mom tried her best to be nice, asking Maggie about Sarah Lawrence and why she'd left, showing old snapshots of me—but the evening was ruined. I thought he would soften up if he could get to know Maggie, see how lovely she is, how gentle. . . . Incredible. To himself, he was the best father in the world because he gave me things, but all I can remember is that he refused to meet my girl. That he turned Rick out of the house. That he missed my graduation. What the hell did I want with all that junk? Cameras, skis, hi-fi sets. I wanted *him*.

Rick is dead in Vietnam—not enough of him left to ship home. I can't think about this. I'll have dinner and go down for cigarettes. Work on the portrait. . . .

No. No. There is a truth hidden here. Like a word you can't find, or a name that goes blank suddenly. I want . . . Go back to the lake, the time you almost drowned. 1955, the same summer. I couldn't swim so I had to wear one of those little orange life jackets. It embarrassed me, yet swimming seemed impossible. We had a boat that summer, a rented one with an outboard, and every day we'd go fishing. Dad was good with mechanical things, boats, cars, but Ben was helpless—couldn't even bait the fish hooks. Was it windy that day? It must have been, because I can remember the boat bobbing by the dock when we climbed in. There was light dancing on the water, like Christmas tinsel scattered on the waves, and the sun was blazing. Nobody put on my life jacket that day—they must have forgotten. Dad started the motor and we headed out to the middle of the lake. I was leaning over the side, trailing my hand in the water and looking for the monster. I was positive that he was down there, and though I was scared of him I wanted to see him. Just once. But all I could see were long grasses swaying, minnows, silver lights. How did it happen? I guess a motorboat passed us too close, because all of a sudden there was a big wave and I screamed and fell over the side. It's so clear . . . that moment of falling. The first thing I felt was the icy shock. Then I plunged downward with my eyes open. It must have only been a second, but the sense of drowning was fantastic, endless. Dad dove in and the next thing I felt was his arms dragging me to the surface. Sunlight hit me in the face and I saw Mom standing up in the boat, waving her arms. Ben was fumbling with the motor. Dad kept shouting to him that I was OK, but Mom was hysterical. Then . . . I don't know. He must have swum to shore with me. I remember being stretched out on the beach while someone gave me artificial respiration. I vomited a little and felt better. I didn't know what had happened, and I wasn't upset till I saw Mom's face. It was twisted in this horrible way and she was crying. . . . I began to cry too, but Leo stopped me. "Now come on," he said. "You're not gonna cry, are you? Aren't you Daddy's

big boy?" He was grinning like it was all a joke—
like I had fallen into the water on purpose—so we both
began to laugh. "That's right!" he said. "That's my little
mensch. Wasn't he brave, Ben? Went right down into
the water and didn't cry." Mother dried me with a towel
and smoothed back my hair, and I felt very important
. . . (We buried the bird in the yard. In a shoebox.
Leo started to walk away, but I said that I wanted a stone
for the grave. He shook his head at me, like he always
did, but went and got a flat stone. And then he wrote *Bird*
on the stone with one of my crayons and I felt better.)

They carried me back to the bungalow and gave me
a warm bath and some soup, and put me to bed. I felt so
happy lying there, as though I had been through a great
adventure—Mister Bear clutched in my arms, my face
tingling from sun and bright water, the cool sheets. I
could hear them in the other room, miles away yet close
enough for sureness, and they were saying how brave I
was, what a good boy I was. Dad began to talk about the
future. . . . My whole childhood is wrapped up in the
sound of his voice talking about the future. I would be
handsome when I grew up, a lady-killer. I would go to
college and major in Business and be a success. He was so
ignorant of who I really was. He watched me grow up and
couldn't believe his eyes, because I seemed deformed. If
he had had other kids it wouldn't have been so bad—but
I became an obsession. "Look, I want to settle this once
and for all. I don't say that painting isn't a good hobby.
Some very nice people paint for relaxation. But for a living? Don't be stupid, you'll starve in a week." (I didn't
starve, Leo. I had my own show last year. To which
everyone came but you.) "What's with the poetry? A nice

day outside and you sit in the house writing poetry. Wake up, Davy. This is the real world." If he said that once, he said it a million times: Wake up, this is the real world. ("The world is inside you," Rick said. And we sat by the Soldiers and Sailors Monument and watched the river. We opened our Math books but couldn't concentrate because the light was so strange. Black water, white tugboats, amber sky. After a while we began to draw, and then for no reason at all he looked at me and said that the world was inside me.) I can't forgive you for what you did to him, Leo. And now he's dead and I can never make it up to him. I hope you rot in your grave for a thousand years.

That dream I had after the drowning incident . . . it stayed with me for a long time. I was standing by the lake, and once again I saw a dancing light on the water. Tinsel scattered on the waves. I dove into the water and gasped—because there, far below me, was a Christmas tree. It was lit with candles and stood on the floor of the lake. I wondered how candles could burn in the water. Then I swam down into the icy greenness, my hands reaching for toys, lights, ornaments. But when I landed on the bottom I went sick with fear, because the Christmas tree was a dragon who breathed fire. His head was wrapped in tinsel and his eyes glowed like lamps and . . . there were dead birds at his feet. Far above me Mom was calling in the sunshine, but I couldn't answer her. I couldn't move. The monster came towards me—and then —though I had been able to breathe before, I stopped breathing. I started to drown. I screamed.

Dad ran into the room. "A thing!" I screamed. "A bad thing!" No, he said, it was only a nightmare, only a dream. "I saw it, Daddy!" It's all right, he said, it's all right. Mom came to the door looking frightened, but Dad said it was nothing, I had had a nightmare. He came over and put his arms around me and I buried my face in his neck. I smelled the shaving lotion and the cigars, and I dug my nails into his flesh, feeling connected to his body, his smell. . . . It was because you fell into the water, he said, that's why you had the bad dream. "But I didn't cry." No, sweetheart, you're a brave boy and you didn't cry. "There was a tree in the water, Daddy." I know, I know. "And then it turned into a bad thing." So, now it's over, everything is all right. . . . He talked until my head fell back on the pillow, but I still held onto his hand. He just kept talking softly, holding my hand. And his hands are buried now in Brooklyn. . . . Mom left the room and we were alone, me half asleep, and he talking in this gentle monotonous voice. He told me a story. He said I was a good boy. He said that he loved me. And I knew . . . I knew that for the rest of my life he would come when there was danger. A million miles could separate us, but he would come and find me—even in the depths of the lake—and we would shoot to the surface together, the silver flying from our hair. And then I was asleep and not asleep, wrapped in his voice like a cloak, and feeling the twilight enter the room and smelling the pine trees outside. But I still held onto his hand, his hands that are buried now, and I felt him over me like a great presence, like the presence of God. And then I fell asleep, with him holding my hand, this man who was my father. . . .

FIVE DAYS AND STILL THE SAME: a bitter taste in my mouth, an anger. Time doesn't move. I'm still sitting in the funeral parlor watching my uncle and my mother like a casual observer. They sat there in grief-stricken silence while I kept having these crazy thoughts —wondering if the coffin was waterproof and what suit Leo was wearing. Amazing. Here was my father lying in a wooden box beneath a blanket of roses, and my main feeling was triumph that I hadn't had a haircut. As though he could still see me, still press five bucks in my hand for the barber. Music was being piped into the room, a sort of religious Muzak, and that made me think of the Beatles and Maggie and the first night I slept with her. I kept trying to push these thoughts away, but the harder I tried the wilder they became: What will happen when all the land is used up? Will they shoot the dead into orbit? Celestial cemeteries? Grief on the launching pad? (OK, Smithers, let's begin the countdown for the funeral. Ten, nine, eight, seven, six . . .) I laughed—and Ben looked at me in horror.

Daddy, my roller skate is broken. Daddy, let's go to the park. Can we see a movie tonight? Leo dear, don't forget the dry cleaning. Dolly, will you please stop worrying so much? Look Davy, if I told you once. . . . I hear so many voices, but most of all I hear him shouting at me the night I left home. "If you think you're taking that phonograph, mister, you're wrong. *I* paid for that machine. And you can just leave those suits in the closet. We'll give them to someone who appreciates them. You think you're gonna get money from me? Not one cent, mister! You can starve for all I care."

Mom tried to reason with him, but he just kept pacing back and forth while I packed. "Sure, sure, take the sweater from Saks Fifth Avenue. Impress your crummy friends with it. Where do you think you're gonna live? On the sidewalk? I thank God Ben isn't here to see this, it would kill him. What's the matter with you—I never treated you right? You didn't have everything you want? Clothes, books, records? Who tortured you here?"

Run, David. Run to the elevator, run to the subway, run to Marty Brooks' apartment. Run, run, never go back, because he is a terrible man, more terrible than

(*18*)

anyone knows. You can hate him now, this dictator who wants to spoil your life, who wants to twist you in his own sick image, this hypocrite. . . . No, not always. Not in the beginning. If I could find what changed him I could find everything. Because he used to be . . . beautiful. Strange. I thought he was a king, a hero, and our Saturdays were so precious to me that I would mark the days off on the calendar. He took me to the circus, a ringside box, and the clown tried to sit on my lap. He bought me a kitten in a pet store. Not the Persian kind he liked, but the one I wanted: black with a skinny tail. When I was nine he took me to the Metropolitan. I was so overwhelmed by the paintings that he promised to take me to the Modern Museum too—"Where the far-out pictures are"—and I thought he was the best father in the world. But even then something was bothering him. He was more critical. . . . Once I told him how some kid in my class was good at Arithmetic and he said, "Make friends with him. Maybe it'll rub off." That hurt me terribly, but a few days later I won the poster contest at school and he was proud. I can't put it all together. . . . I remember being nine because of the apartment on 73rd Street. It must have been shabby but I liked the smallness of it, the cooking smells. There were bikes and sleds in the hallway and you could hear everybody's lives through the air shaft. Frankie and I used to drop things down there, and it was exciting to hear them echo on the bottom. Mom liked the place too, even though the kitchen was small. She kept a bunch of plants on the windowsill. . . .

Pale, silent woman—I can still see you watering

those plants in your bathrobe, the first thing you did every morning. Singing along with the radio as you made breakfast. Happy in those days. But after we moved to Riverside Drive . . . doormen, a fountain in the lobby, that awful chandelier. And those cocktail parties for the buyers: everyone getting plastered and telling dirty jokes. You accepted it. Why? What power did he have over you? After he bought the business he would come home late for supper, and if the meal wasn't hot he would get up and leave the room—slamming the door behind him. And you would be afraid. . . . I wanted to yell at you: Stand up to him! Walk out! Throw the food in his face! But the meaner he was, the more you'd apologize. Yes dear, I know it was my fault. No dear, I won't do it again. Yet on 73rd Street I remember him bringing you flowers, giving you money for the beauty parlor even when times were hard. "Never mind what it costs. Get a manicure too. The works." It's like a kaleidoscope, images shifting, fragments. . . . It would stay light till eight o'clock in the summer, and after dinner I would take my roller skates and go down to meet Frankie. We would skate around the block, not allowed to cross the street, but around and around, daring each other to skate on one foot, to jump over cracks. And the last light would be burning in the sky and we could hear tugboats on the river. . . . I loved the bakery shops on Broadway and the Jewish delicatessens. Old men sitting in the sun, little dogs on leashes, movie houses. But he spoke of the "bad element" that was coming into the neighborhood, the blacks, the Puerto Ricans. And so he got out of that neighborhood where there was so much life—and died.

Mom wanted me to take his gold cufflinks ("You should have something that was your father's, Davy.") but I left them on the bureau. How could I tell her that what I had was more durable than gold: nineteen years of despair. Horrible—sorting out his possessions, deciding where things should go. I stood in the monument company while Mom chose marble, thinking, don't use marble. Let me make a column of jewelry and car bumpers. Cufflinks and bumpers from the Buick, his watch with the diamond chips, two Sulka ties, one Sony radio, and a golf club stuck on the top like a flag. (What do you want for your birthday? I asked Rick. "For you to be happy," he said. And I was embarrassed and laughed.) We were poor on 73rd Street, but I never knew it. All I knew was that I loved my room with the blackboard on the wall and the little desk where I would pretend to write stories. If I leaned out of the window I could see the river, and the breeze smelled of salt and coal. I would lie in bed at night listening to the traffic, and New York was like a big machine pounding and throbbing in the darkness. So strange and secret to be a child, with everything new, sound, sight, taste, one's own warm body. . . . Ben had even less than we in his apartment uptown, but he was indifferent to possessions. And Dad —critical of him for working at the Library of Jewish Studies. You had put him through college and now the investment wasn't paying off. Right, Leo? You never saw his gentleness or the poetry in him, just a bad investment. When I was twelve and began going to temple with him, you took me aside. "Look, I've nothing against the Jewish religion. But what I want is that you should choose your own religion when you're older. That way, you won't feel pressured." What you meant was: Don't be like your uncle, don't borrow problems. Assimilate, make friends with those nice Protestants at your school.

What changed this man? It was . . . no, more than money. More than success. A dissatisfied quality, a vast irritability with his place in the world. I don't know . . . but I remember the day he became partners with Shulman. One of our Saturdays together. He said that we were going to do something special and then meet Mom and Ben for lunch. He had an announcement to make to us, something very exciting. . . . We took the bus downtown, and it seemed to me that I had never seen him so happy. He kept making jokes and ruffling my hair. Finally we got to St. Mark's Place and began to walk east, holding hands like we always did, and suddenly I was disappointed. Because the neighborhood we were walking through was a slum. (The same neighborhood I live in now. It's all a circle, Leo. You escaped from this place and I returned to it. To find freedom. To groove on life as it is—raw, chaotic, messy. What would you have said if someone had told you that your little boy would wind up in your old neighborhood with a bunch of "weirdos," freaking on acid? What would you have thought?)

It seemed alien to me then: crowded streets, pushcarts, garbage, people screaming out of windows at their kids. There was a bad smell in the air and a couple of drunks were lying in a doorway. My disappointment was so strong that I had to hold back the tears, because I had thought we were going to a museum. . . . He stopped in

(22)

front of a building and looked up at it. The expression on his face was odd, so I looked too, but it was only a faded brick tenement. The stoop was broken and there were bags of garbage in the hall. "Davy," he said, "this is the house where I was born." I didn't understand at first because it seemed so strange. How come you were born here? I asked.

He touched my cheek and sighed. *"Shaifeleh,* maybe you're too young to understand this. I don't know. Maybe I should have waited till later. But I wanted you to see this neighborhood so you could get a picture of how I grew up. You think it's bad now? Believe me, years ago it was worse. Yet my father came to this country with high hopes." Then he started to tell me a story—about his father and the persecution he had known in Poland. How he had been so glad to come to America that he had kissed the hand of the immigration officer at Ellis Island. And how he had thought New York was a place of shining opportunity. "But he wound up a peddler on a street corner, Davy, and in ten years he looked like an old man. Opportunity? The only opportunity my father found was a kick in the backside. He couldn't speak the language and the only trade he knew was farming. So to complicate his troubles he got married, and by the time I was born the spirit had gone out of him: an old Jew who left for work at dawn and came home limping. We lived in the basement, right down there, and after the others came from Poland we slept four in a bed. I never had a childhood. My first memory is lying awake at night because of the rats." . . . He went on and on, his face tense with emotion—and I was embarrassed. I didn't know why he was telling me this. It sounded so corny, like a bad film. When he got older he told that story on every family occasion, as though he were proud of it, but there was nothing to be proud of because his father was a fool. Borrowing money all the time, buying lottery tickets, trying to support his relatives. They stole him blind . . . one, in fact, even took his gold watch, the only decent thing he owned, and pawned it. A charming family. Yet to Leo it was a very heroic story, the saga of the immigrant in MGM technicolor. . . . "You can't imagine what it was like. Every morning my father would make me follow the milkman's horse with a bucket, to pick up the manure. Even manure could be sold for something, a few pennies, so I did this terrible thing and then went to school smelling bad. Hunger? I was so hungry that I would go into restaurants and steal ketchup from the tables. You, my darling—you want an ice cream soda, Mother gives you a quarter. But to me and Ben a piece of sugar was a treat. Toys, candy, we had none of those things, and I never got a present in my life."

It was November, and the day was so clear that the city seemed washed in cold water. Beyond the pushcarts and the crowds I could see skyscrapers uptown, ice-blue and silver, green and gold. And suddenly I wanted to draw those buildings. That need came over me all the time—to have a pencil in my hand, a crayon—but I never talked about it. I had changed, shyer, more secretive, scared. Of what? I would hide the toys I liked in the back of the closet, as though Dad were going to. . . . There are too many memories. I can't find him. I kept that Raggedy Andy doll in the closet for years. Wrong to play with dolls, a boy playing with dolls. . . . *But I want to find him.* I look in the mirror and see Leo's face. I put my coat on like him, walk like him. ("He looks just like his father, doesn't he?") Once we had our picture taken on Broadway—the spitting image, Davy—and I wanted to scream, no, no, I'm just me, let me alone! ("You've never looked at him," Rick said. "You've never even seen him.") Go back. I was staring at the skyscrapers, but his voice wove in and out of my consciousness: "So the years passed and I watched my father become a silent man. Watched Ben's eyes go bad because we couldn't afford glasses. Watched my mother take from her plate every night and put something on my father's, trying to keep him alive. It drove me crazy—the way she was starving herself for him—so one morning I ran out of the house and got a job. Left grammar school and went to work in a factory. In ten years I was helping them all: Ben in college, food on the table, my mother with her first warm coat. She had never had roast beef, my mother, and the night I brought one home she held it in her lap and cried. And *that* was America to me—this thing I had accomplished."

People on the street were staring at him, he was so worked up, but my mind drifted away. It was such a beautiful morning, like crystal, the city poised and clear. There were pigeons flying towards the East River. Dark against the sun, then light. Down the street a peddler was crying Day-O, Day-O, and I wondered what it meant. I was daydreaming, lost, wrapped in the weather, a part of the distance . . . and then . . . one minute he was talking and the next minute he had grabbed my collar. *"What's the matter with you?* Why don't you listen when I talk?"* I don't know, I said, I'm sorry. "Sorry isn't good enough! I try to tell you something, and you day-dream. What's the matter with you? You think it's pleas-ant for me to come back to this neighborhood? You think I enjoy telling this story?" He was so angry that he was trembling, but I didn't know what I had done. I had for-gotten to listen, that was all, yet his face was mur-derous. Christ, how could I have known what the story meant to him? I was nine years old. Giving me all this melodramatic crap. . . . We stood there—Leo trembling, and me pressed up against a hydrant—and for a second I thought he was going to hit me. But he let go of my collar and turned away. Then he started up the street without me and I felt panicky, abandoned, ashamed of what I had done though ignorant of what I had done . . . and I ran after him.

Sunday. And I love you Maggie, sitting there staring at your portrait. There's not a bit of vanity in your face as you look at it. Just curiosity. Wondering why I chose those forms, those colors. Beneath the colors—light. I have reversed you, putting the sadness on the outside and the light within. No one else sees you this way. To other people you are cheerful, transparent, a person without se-crets. But I know your sadness and illumine it. . . . When I woke up today I realized something. My paint-ing was a threat to Dad. Science, Math, History: I could have been a genius in those fields, eccentric. But art was dangerous, and the more my work improved the more he objected. Using crazy excuses, like it was bad for my eyes, I wasn't getting enough fresh air. Almost as though . . . he were jealous. I remember the time Mr. Cummings sent a note home with my report card, saying I had talent. Leo brushed it aside. "That's all very nice, but I'm more interested in your grades. A C-average isn't good enough for Dartmouth." His obsession with that place . . . making me apply early, driving me to New Hampshire. ("You see? A gorgeous campus.") And he made such a fool of himself with the Director of Admissions, calling him "Doctor" and opening the door for him. He got all his rich friends to write letters of recommendation, and even tried to bribe the Headmaster at school. "Listen, don't worry. We'll just make a little contribution to the school, and your grades will go up." You mean, *bribe* them? I asked. "Who's talking about a bribe? All I said was a little contribution. For the scholarship fund." By little he meant five thousand dollars. I was so upset that I phoned Ben, who said not to worry, that the school wouldn't do such a thing. But it was my first knowledge of how corrupt Leo was. No, my second. . . .

You weren't like that in the old days. When you talked about the business you had a certain purity. Shulman was cheating on his income tax, keeping phony books, and it wasn't right. Shulman ordered cheap goods and tried to pass them off as quality. If it were *your* outfit. . . . The minute it was your outfit you did the same things: lied, cheated, paid off the buyers, sold dresses for cash. And Shulman wound up a broken old man, retired, and begging you to let him visit the office—just so he could have someplace to go. "Incredible," you said to

Mom. "This idiot calls me on the phone and asks if he can't come in mornings and sit at his old desk. Look, I told him, I'm not running a recreation center. For a little recreation, play golf." Yet your own feelings were so sensitive that you would brood all day if I forgot to say good morning. Once we had a date to go to a ballgame, and I forgot and went to the library—and you were so hurt that you didn't talk to me for a week. You lousy hypocrite. You thought there was one law for me and another for you. If I told a lie all hell broke loose, but for you everything was possible. Your biggest joke was: Do like I say, not like I do. ("OK, sonny," you said to Rick. "That's it, everything's over. Now, out! *Out of this house.*" You pushed him against a table and clutched his shirt, your face white with rage. And I couldn't believe what was happening, couldn't believe that. . . . Eight months later his helicopter crashed and there wasn't enough for a coffin. Everything burnt to ashes. While you lay by the pool. While Mom and Ben went to a matinée. While his parents bought a new car. Everyone ate and slept and grew fat—while he burned.)

That day on the Lower East Side . . . we walked over to Ratner's for lunch, and Leo didn't say a word until we were about to go in. Then he put his hand on my shoulder. "There's just one thing I want you to remember. Everything I have planned in my life is for you." I nodded as though I understood what he meant—and then we were inside the restaurant, Mom waving to us from the corner. Dad's mood had changed like lightning, and he made a big point of kissing her and shaking hands with Ben. I hated the way he acted in restaurants . . . snapping his fingers for the waiter, asking stupid questions about the food. . . . What's the occasion? Ben asked. "You'll see," he said. "Davy, if you eat the vegetables, you'll get two desserts." He was drumming his fingers on the table and smiling, and Mom couldn't understand it. Where did you and Davy go this morning?" she asked. "Darling, that's a secret. Well, Benjamin, how's the book?" Ben looked surprised because Dad never asked about his writing, but after a second he said that it was going well—that it would be finished in a few years. "A few *years?* In a few years we may be dead. Why don't you write something easy?" Ben laughed and said that easy writing made hard reading. Leo didn't get it. "This is 1959. Who wants to read about the Warsaw Ghetto? You have talent, Ben, you could make money . . ." (And now you're dead and Benjamin is still writing. He won't ever finish the book, but it doesn't matter. You criticized him, made him feel inadequate, but if you'd ever known him you would have known that the book was his life. He used to read chapters to me and they were fantastic, but then he'd have to revise, and revise again—cutting, rearranging, making footnotes. His perfectionism drove you mad, and you were annoyed whenever I praised him. "What's going on with this family? Writers, painters, a whole bunch of bohemians I've got." Bohemians. Hippies. Degenerates. And I look at Ben's portrait on my wall and see the face of Elijah.)

Dad rapped on the table. Everyone looked up. He paused, he cleared his throat, he took Mom's hand. Then he announced that he and Shulman were becoming partners. . . . Their voices are only echoes, I don't remember the words. Something about him putting in ten thousand, great plans for the future—Mom's face shocked, because ten thousand was their life's savings—Ben staring blankly at the tablecloth. . . . It took me years to understand what he'd done. Shulman didn't want a partner, but since the business was failing he had no choice. Real Mafia tactics on Dad's part. Ten thousand was nothing for a stake in that outfit, but Shulman couldn't pay his creditors and was afraid his wife would find out. Had swallowed sleeping pills in the men's room when the collection agency came around. The poor bastard. Pressured by Leo and no other way out. And all for a measly ten thousand. Nothing illegal about it. Just a callousness, a greed, a very well-wrought and accurate plan to take away another man's work and make it his own. . . . My rich and successful father.

Ben cleared his throat and said that the plan seemed a little risky. Leo laughed. "Risky? Everything's risky. Listen, you think it's fun being a salesman? Bowing and scraping to people, taking all kinds of *dreck* from the buyers? Well, those days are over." He glanced around the table, waiting for everyone to praise him. But Mom and Ben were stunned by the idea, and I was too young to understand it. "Hey," he said. "What is this, a funeral? Why the long faces?" We're just worried, Mom said quietly. God, the way he exploded. . . . People turned in their chairs. Yelling at her that she didn't appreciate him, that she didn't care about their future, that she didn't care about me. Then he turned on Ben, saying that he had no ambition. How could *he* understand such a break when he'd never had ambition of his own. . . . On and on, till he finally left the table and went to the washroom. (Why do I suddenly remember this? The nights when you worked late and I couldn't sleep for fear you had had an accident. If it got past nine o'clock I would start crying to myself because I thought a car had run you over. I could see it all—you crossing the dark street, the car screaming out from nowhere. You, my father, being taken to a hospital, nobody knowing your name.)

It wasn't my fault! He dug his own grave, no matter what they said. ("Everything he's doing is for you. Don't you know that?") He would come home from the office looking like a ghost, have dinner, and take his work into the bedroom. Work till midnight and get up at six. Go back to the office and come home again tired. He worked on Saturdays, holidays. ("The whole burden's on my shoulders. Shulman's no help.") Your father's killing himself, I'm worried about him. What was *I* supposed to do? I didn't want him to work so hard. I didn't even understand it. The man's killing himself, I never saw anyone work that way. ("Davy, someday this business will be yours. You'll walk into it like royalty.") So I dreamed of running away and being a hobo, a wanderer. Nobody's son, nobody's child. . . . What do you want to be when you grow up? Frankie asked me. "A person who rides freight trains," I said. Freedom, the long wail of trains in the Hudson Valley. I would dream of hopping a freight and going to Kansas. Dust bowls and cyclones, flat lands without skyscrapers, dry earth. You can walk for a day and not see anyone, and the plains go on for a thousand miles. . . . I didn't like his office, yet he took me there all the time. ("You want to play with the typewriter? Go on, sweetheart.") Soot drifting down from the smokestacks, a veil of it on everything. Racks of dresses, the models walking around in their slips. Dirty jokes, coffee in cardboard containers, phones ringing. I wandered through those rooms in despair, hating the dresses, the jokes, the people. ("What a handsome kid. He could be a movie star. Put him in the movies, Leo.") Laughter, cigarette smoke, people eating at their desks. And him—showing me off. ("What do you think of this boy? He's going to private school next year.") The men's room was dirty and I didn't like using it, but he would always take me there before we went to lunch. Seventh Avenue swarmed like an anthill: groups of men arguing on the sidewalk, boys pushing racks of clothes through the street. At last I would be home, safe. Off with the blue suit, into my corduroy pants, and down to meet Frankie. Where were you all day? "My father's office." No kidding, what do you do there? "Oh, everything. It's neat." What's your father, a salesman? "No, a doctor. He operates on people." Why did I lie about him all the time? Eighth grade, everyone talking about their fathers, and me saying that Leo was in the publishing business.

But you were only a merchant, my dear father, and you had the merchant's disease: complaining. If you got a big order it wasn't big enough. If one of your stocks split you would complain that the others hadn't. Nothing was ever good enough for you. I would make presents for your birthday, little paintings on cardboard, and then not give them to you. Buy a bottle of shaving lotion instead. . . . Why couldn't you see life as it was? To you, life was something to be managed, a big universal shop where you

(*32*)

were boss. That was so funny—the day I tried to explain Zen to you. "How can a person *do* something without doing something?" you asked. It's reality itself, I said patiently, nothing to do with action. You looked at me like I was feebleminded. "I never heard such nonsense. People *do* things. They don't sit around staring at their navels." What was the point? I took you to the theater—Genet—and you left at the intermission. "If I want filth, I can buy it on 42nd Street." And I came home from school one day to find my room changed. Everything piled in the closet: books, records, easel, the photo of Rick. I was so angry that I was afraid to face you, fearing that I would knock you down. Mom helped me put everything back the next morning, but it took me a long time to realize the meaning of that act. You altered my room with the hope of altering me.

(Alter me, change me, cut me to your mold. Laugh at my ideas, make fun of what I love. Burst into my room and turn the phonograph down. Eye my poetry collection suspiciously: Poetry? A grown boy? Send me to the barber, buy my clothes, choose my schools and friends. Take my phone calls: Who did you say this is? What's the name again? Lay down rules, ten o'clock curfew, twelve on weekends. Enter the bathroom without knocking. Tease me when I shave. . . . No good, no good at all. I still became myself. In the face of ridiculous, impossible odds—became myself.)

We sat in the restaurant, everyone caught in his own silence. Ben reading the menu, Mom staring at the table, me watching the traffic outside. I felt lonely, disconnected, so I slipped into my Secret Place. It was completely real to me, this checkerboard land where I could step from square to square. Blue for oceans, me the captain of a tugboat. Gold for the desert, Arabs gliding over hot sand. Green for jungles where crazy-colored birds swooped from trees. Black? For the night, I guess, when I could fly through a tangle of stars and see comets falling to earth. . . . And I am not a real boy, but someone from another planet who has been mistakenly adopted by Leo and Dolly Marks. Someone with a secret mission, so that I must pretend to be an earthchild who plays baseball and does homework and watches television. I have learned their language the better to deceive them. But when the time comes, I shall rise from my bed on 73rd Street and fly through the window emitting secret high frequency signals—fly over the Hudson and into the stars, my brain having recorded all sorts of information for the war that will blow up the world. And looking down I will see these people called the Marks leaning frantically out of the window. Davy! Come back, come back. . . . Then Leo was at the table again and I woke up.

He had been in the men's room a long time, and the three of us glanced at him wondering if he was still mad. But he was so calm you would have thought nothing had happened. His hair was slicked down and his face looked as though he had washed it. He asked if anyone wanted more coffee, and got up to pay the check. I trailed after him like I always did and we stood in line at the cashier's desk. I watched him study the check, adding each item to be sure he hadn't been cheated, his lips moving silently, and then it came over me like a wave: the knowledge of his disappointment. He had taken me to the house where he was born and I hadn't listened to his story. He had made a big announcement at lunch and no one had reacted. He had done something important in the world and nobody cared. Suddenly I could have wept for him, this man who wanted approval so much, who always sweated when he talked and mopped his face with a handkerchief. . . . He gave me a little smile. "What are you thinking, my *chachem?*" And I knew that this was my chance to make everything all right. He was my father and I loved him and I had the power to heal his wounds. Had always had that power. Not Mom, not Benjamin, but me—the wizard of happiness. He ruffled my hair. "Cat got your tongue?" (Say something! Say you're sorry, say that you love him, make him feel better.) To my horror, I turned away and pretended to watch something outside, all the words unspoken . . . and the moment was lost. I could feel his bewilderment like a hand on my shoulder. And for a second I was caught between two worlds. What was I thinking? I couldn't have known that within a few years he would be a stranger to me, that I would learn to despise everything he stood for, that he would become a caricature of the person I loved. . . .

He paid the check and an invisible wall dropped between us. Concrete.

L AST NIGHT I WOKE UP with this fear inside me. I don't
know what it was. The night was cool and Maggie
was sleeping quietly, but my heart was pounding. I
went and sat by the window. Nothing. A few cars passing
by, some kids standing in a doorway, a girl singing in the
street. But it was like . . . the world emptied of light forever. As though dawn wouldn't come, as though the street
would remain paralyzed like a Balthus painting. The kids
would never grow old and the singer would never stop
her song—I believed this and was afraid. I smoked some
grass and things got softer and moved again, a little cat

slinking in the darkness, a sudden cloud across the sky
. . . and for the first time since he died, I felt him close
to me. Why wasn't it strange? I could almost reach out
and touch him, yet the whole thing seemed natural. Like
the New Year's Eve we sat up together drinking beer and
watching the snow outside. Mom had gone to bed, but
Leo and I kept sitting in the darkness listening to a band
on the radio. The snow was drifting down like feathers,
soft piles of it on the terrace. When midnight comes, I
thought, he'll kiss me. But at twelve o'clock he just patted
my shoulder and told me to go to bed.

Count the days and wait to recover. Paint pictures,
play records, make love. Time will heal. . . . It doesn't.
A popular myth. I should be dancing on his grave, rejoic-
ing that he can't hurt me anymore, yet all I seem to do is
relive things. The funeral, the luncheon, Arnie Lowenstein's hypocritical voice . . .

I never knew a man who loved his family so much.

It's true, Arnold. He was wonderful to us.

Everywhere he went—out would come the snapshots of you and Davy.

I know.

A beautiful person. And such a sense of humor.
That time in Atlantic City, remember?

But he worked so hard. It broke my heart.

Well, look, he got what he wanted from life. And to
do that, a man has to work. Dolly, forgive me for
asking—but he left you well provided?

(*37*)

Very well, Arnold, and a pension for old Mr. Warner.

He got what he wanted from life. Two color televisions and a Buick. A cashmere coat and a set of golf clubs. Nirvana. The Lowensteins were on their third glass of brandy, feeling no pain, and Ben was nodding at everything they said. Mom seemed grateful for the lies they were telling. Arnie kept glancing at me, not knowing how to bring me into the conversation and wondering how his best friend's son had turned into a freak from the East Village. Finally he coughed and said, "Well, kiddo. How are things, uh, downtown?" I gave him a marijuana smile and whispered, "Groovy," confirming his worst suspicions. The dining room seemed so small. . . . When I was twelve it seemed huge, but now it was just an ugly little room with heavy furniture, and too much silver on the sideboard, and the smell of a thousand meals in the carpet. Blink your eyes and he's there: a fork in his left hand, a pencil in his right. Working at the table while he eats, belching, talking with his mouth full. A Very Beautiful Person.

Arnie was getting sloppy, sentimental. I knew that if I didn't get out of there I'd throw the brandy in his face —so I got up from the table and went to my room. I couldn't believe my eyes . . . because nothing had been changed. Exactly the same as I'd left it: the Tchelitchew print over the bed, my poetry collection spilling out of the bookcase, records everywhere, my brown sweater on the floor. (And this, folks, is a shrine to a teen-ager who ran away. His father comes here every night and lights a candle.) He probably did too. Probably sat in that room every night grieving for the prodigal son. No. What he really did was rifle the place, looking for secret diaries, dope, pornography, muttering wildly to himself, "Hippies, hippies." Such sad useless paranoid crap. . . . I was squarer than you were, Leo, and you never saw it. You at least were colorful, a throwback to your Hassidic ancestors who got drunk and danced in the fields of Poland. But I had WHITE MIDDLE-CLASS AMERICAN stamped on my forehead in ink, and when I headed for the Village it was in a Brooks Brothers shirt with a Mark Cross suitcase under my arm. Insane. Square little David sitting in the East Village with his modest supply of grass, everyone else on acid, and his father screaming into the telephone, "If you don't come back here, I'm gonna have you arrested! A beautiful young boy on *drugs*. How is such a thing possible?"

My room . . . so strange and so familiar. Yes, I wore that sweater, bought those records, slept in that bed and used that comb, but in another life. . . . I couldn't stop staring at things, touching them. I folded the sweater and put it in a drawer, put a few records away, looked in my desk. Some letters from Marty, an old calendar. A valentine from Mom. Then I wondered if Mister Bear was still in the closet, and he was, and I started to cry.

(Observe, Mr. Lowenstein: the hippie is crying. Sitting on his bed holding a teddy bear. Not even stoned, which would be a good excuse, but crying over a teddy bear with one eye and a paw stained with grape juice. Isn't that interesting? He is practically human. Wind him up and he will laugh, cry, or pour you a cocktail. Put a penny in him and he will bow and shake hands. Replace his batteries and he might even get a haircut. Isn't that cute? Only $5.95.)

Overnight. One minute on 73rd Street, poor—the next minute in a big apartment by the river. All of a sudden doormen were opening doors for us and hailing cabs. All of a sudden we had a maid. . . . The lobby smelled of disinfectant and I hated the purple rug, the chandelier. But to Leo it was class: an apartment with a terrace, river view. Mom walked through those rooms like a ghost, cleaning ashtrays, straightening pillows, but there was nothing for her to do because of Bessie. So she began making her own clothes, but he stopped that. "What nonsense is this? Five charge accounts you've got." Overnight we had turned into the people we were not—and the masks were stuck. My first memory of that place is Dad working through dinner, making lists of figures at the table. He hated Shulman now, and every meal was a series of complaints about his stupidity. When he got tired of criticizing Max, he would turn on Mom. Why couldn't she handle the maid better? Why was the food never hot? Why didn't she wear her hair different? "Ten bucks a week for the beauty parlor, and you look worse than the *schvartzeh*." Her whole life had been based on taking care of us, cooking, cleaning, and now those things were gone. He wouldn't even let her go to the supermarket because a place on Broadway delivered. In desperation she started playing bridge with Mrs. Shulman's friends, going to matinées, taking one cocktail too many—and the migraines began. Our life had become a reproduction on the grand scale, everything fake. Renaissance chairs, Georgian tables, Romanesque cupboards. The history of the world bought on credit and jammed into six rooms. Did it look old? Buy it! Did Shulman have one? Buy two! Buy, buy, buy. Give yourself background, lineage. . . . Why shouldn't she have given up? A small-town girl from Virginia dumped into a nouveau riche nightmare.

Suddenly I was thirteen, either giggling hysterically or so depressed I couldn't speak. Locking myself in my room to read dirty books. Sending away for pimple creams. Listening to Brahms and crying. . . . Go more slowly. Try to see it. Because that first onslaught of sex was like a disease, a madness, and every time I masturbated I would wait for God to strike me. Lethal, getting sex and religion all at once, and convinced that I was the only person in the world who felt that way. Other people *couldn't* feel that way because they walked through the streets calm and sober and serene. But I—the madman— thought of nothing but sexual intercourse and committed obscenities in my room. Lord, make me pure and I will be your servant. Please, dear Lord, take these evil thoughts away. A thirteen-year-old schizophrenic: trotting off to private school in a neat blue blazer, going to temple on Saturdays with Ben, perfect table manners, but at night—a degenerate. Did Leo help? This great man of the world? Of course not. Feed and clothe your child, educate him and vaccinate him, but *do not* mention sex. The inevitable happened—he caught me. And it was the only time he ever hit me. Shouting that nice boys didn't do such things, that it ruined your health, sapped your strength, that *nice* boys worked their energy off in sports, that it was a disgusting habit. . . . A week later he walked into my room with a book, *What Every Boy Should Know About Sex,* but it was too late. Because by now I had more guilt than any manual could correct. . . . Oh God, it's all so sad. We come into the world clean and shiny and uncorrupted, simple as beasts, and then they do things to us. Show us how dirty we are. Invent our sins. Break us into segments of clean and unclean. Tear us from our own hands. Snap on the lights.

(And then it was the first time and I was faced with this thing I had never accomplished, with a girl I didn't know. A long-haired dark girl with green eyes and a wide sweet mouth. I had never made it before and when she found this out . . . then I would be a fool, an imbecile who had come on very strong only to disappoint her. A middle-class neurotic, screwed up about sex like his parents. But she couldn't have known these things, so she took off her skirt and sandals and her white blouse, and laughed because we didn't know each other's names . . . and said that her name was Maggie.) Where is the truth? In that night, or in my childhood? Maggie saved me—but before that moment were the corridors of my adolescence, endless hallways smelling of wax and chalk. Criminals in school uniforms. Maniacs posing as schoolboys. At eight-fifteen we would stand in line at the foot of the marble staircase, and the Headmaster would come down to shake hands with each of us. His favorite ritual. "Good morning, sir. Yes, sir. Thank you, sir." Hair plastered down with water, scrubbed faces, blue blazers and gray flannels. High-ceilinged rooms with long tables where I would sit staring out the window, the teacher's voice droning on and on. The vast silence of study hall, kids passing notes. And the cruelty in Central Park that the coach never saw: everyone going for my shins with their hockey sticks because they knew I wouldn't fight back. Marty, one year older, saying, "Never mind them, Dave. *I* like you. Isn't that enough?" It wasn't. I would have died to be popular. Would have died to be in on their secrets, their schemes for cheating, their talk about girls. So I stole a deck of playing cards from Leo's drawer that had naked women on them, and took them to school and gave them away and waited to be popular. . . . The little locker room crucifixions, kids clustering together with plans and me left out. (I'm a freak, a clod, a weirdo, a drip. Lord, please change me. Please make me popular. I'll do anything if you'll make me popular.) Then one day it no longer mattered—because I realized that I was going to be an artist. . . .

And now, Uncle Benjamin, you come into the story —riding on your Talmud, a thousand prophets behind you. Into the story carrying whole synagogues on your back, your gray hair flying in the wind. You—with your glasses and shy smile, who had always been around like the family dog—suddenly became sacred to me. Because you were writing a book. Because you knew more about Judaism than anyone on earth. Because you went to concerts and liked poetry and art, and because . . . you loved me as I was. Maybe it began on the day I discovered Yeats and quoted one of his poems, only to have you finish it. Maybe it was the time we went to the Rodin exhibit, walking silently through the museum, our hands touching. I don't know . . . but on one of those days our souls collided, and after that I couldn't get enough of you. You lived in the midst of this sick world with total serenity, typing your book at the kitchen table and drinking glasses of tea. Playing Bach on an ancient phonograph, books and papers all over the floor. The windows of your apartment were so dirty that you couldn't see the street, but you never noticed. Never noticed the holes in your sweaters or your socks that didn't match. How I loved you . . . your bachelor meals, your long stories from the Midrash, your quiet sense of humor. Once we were walking in the park, and there was a caterpillar in my way and I kicked it aside. "No," you said, "wait a minute." You went back and picked up the caterpillar, who had curled itself into a ball, and showed it to me. Furry and small, with black and yellow stripes. It must have liked the warmth of your hand because it uncurled and stretched itself out.

"It's pretty," I said.

And then you smiled. "One should always know whom one is kicking."

Beneath your humor lay a reverence for life I didn't understand—but you had been 4F in the Second World War while relatives died in Europe, and you could never forget. Saying *Kaddish* with you seemed supernatural, the silent dead reaching to us from their graves. People I had never known, with names like Muni and Felix and Herschel, rose from the ashes at Treblinka. . . . It was amazing to me that the Jews had been put into ovens. Amazing —and unreal.

I would watch your face in temple and light seemed to come from it, your lips parted, the corners of your eyes moist. (Hear, O Israel, the Lord our God, the Lord is One) and I would ask God to make me like you, pious and good. Why is it so special to be a Jew? I asked you once. And you took my hand and said, "Because we have survived. . . ." Strange gentle man, you were kind to my father in ways I couldn't comprehend. Pardoning his faults and looking for his virtues. Listening to his lectures on money while your mind was on literature. Painful, remembering all this . . . my heart tightening whenever the phone rang, walking past the library hoping to see your face in a window. . . . You encouraged me to write poems. Bought me art supplies when my allowance ran out. Took me to the theater when you couldn't afford it—and hung all my drawings in your room. You were so beautifully remote, a man whom the world couldn't touch . . . and though you only lived a few blocks away I wrote you letters like you were in Alaska. So of course Leo went insane. "This fool who can't even earn a living! This dreamer who spends his lifetime writing a book! Wake up, Davy. This is the real world." But the world was you now, Benjamin, because you loved me as I was.

And then the world came crashing down.

(Why do I want to write this? I've gone over it a million times. It should be finished. All kids grow up and become disillusioned and twisted, and survive. Everyone survives—even the madmen. But this thing that happened was the cause of all the later problems, the sexual hangups. . . .) Start at the beginning: a spring night and one of Dad's designers coming to dinner. I dreaded the whole thing because his greatest pleasure these days was to show off what he owned. His wife, his possessions, his son. He made me wear my school blazer, and had Bessie polish the furniture, and ordered Mom to wear her red dress. Didn't ask her, ordered her. And when he came out of the bedroom he was dressed like a banker: sober, conservative. He and Mom had an argument because he said her makeup looked lousy, and that tense look came over her face. . . . Why didn't I pity her? He was destroying her day by day, word by word, yet all I felt was contempt because she wouldn't fight back. He inspected me like a sergeant, top to bottom. "Davy, I want you to be on your best behavior tonight because Anne Fleming is a very special person. A real talent with fabrics and only twenty-eight years old. You'll love her." By this time I was prepared to hate her, but when I went to answer the door a beautiful person was standing there. Black dress, straight blond hair, a very open face. Bessie served cocktails in the den, and all of a sudden I didn't feel the way I usually did with strangers—fat, stupid, shy—because this woman seemed interested in me. She had noticed my watercolors right away and said how good they were. "Yeah," said Leo. "A Michelangelo I've got. But painting's only a hobby—his real talent is Math." I looked at Leo in amazement, but he didn't notice. "Some kid, huh? Head of his class and captain of the hockey team. You should see the report cards he brings home." I could feel my face getting red, so I got up and walked over to the window, ashamed.

I can still see the table that night, polished like a mirror, plates with pink roses on them, pink napkins. And Leo, talking with his mouth full. "Now take Max Shulman. A well-meaning person, but ignorant. You know what I mean? No class. A bargain basement mentality." Anne was listening politely to all this, but Mom

(46)

was a million miles away. Leo hadn't brought her into the conversation once and I almost felt sorry for her. She did have too much makeup on, and compared to Anne she seemed old-fashioned. Eventually the two of them discovered that they had relatives in Virginia, so they talked about this until Dad interrupted. "Dolly comes from a very old family in Richmond. Father owned a pharmaceutical company." And that was the last straw—because Mom's father had owned a little drugstore that had gone broke during the Depression. I don't know why this hit me so hard, but I felt like bursting into tears. He did this all the time, lied about us, tried to make us more than we were. It made me feel that Mom and I weren't good enough for him. . . . (How would this have looked under acid? A Day-Glow menagerie: Leo a rhinoceros, Mom a llama, and Anne—a cat. One of those smooth quick jungle cats with every muscle oiled. The jungle is electric-blue with hot sand glimmering under a neon sun. Razor blade leaves. Licorice grass. Within the eye of the cat is a shy little pig—me—and within the eye of the pig are all of them. Mirrors within mirrors, glances spinning and falling. One eye.) The thing that baffled me was that Anne Fleming seemed to like Leo. He was at his worst, yet she laughed at his jokes and listened carefully to everything he said. Bessie served coffee and then Mom asked to be excused. A headache. I shook hands with Anne and went off to do my homework, and as I sat in my room I could hear Leo and her talking business in the den. I was doing Math or General Science, I can't remember which, and after a while I came to a problem I couldn't solve. I didn't know whether to interrupt Dad or not, but since he al-

(47)

ways liked helping me with homework I took my note-book and headed for the den. Mom's door was closed and I could hear Bessie singing in the kitchen.

Now a film in slow-motion. Very slow. I walk down the hall that has black and white checked linoleum, come to the den and pause in the doorway, my notebook under my arm. Leo and Anne Fleming are sitting on the red couch facing each other. They are not talking. Instead, Leo is holding her chin in his hand and staring into her eyes. He is holding her chin as one would hold a child's, but the look on his face is not fatherly. It is a look I have never seen before. Her face is worshipful, her eyes search-ing his, a grateful smile on her mouth, as though . . . he were a king and she his subject. As though she would do anything he asked. Their brandy glasses have not been touched, and for some reason the TV is playing without sound. Slowly, gently, he begins to trace her lips with his finger . . . I step quickly into the hall, go back to my room, close the door and sit down at my desk. I concen-trate on the problem again, Math or General Science, and work on it for at least five minutes.

Then I begin to shake.

I understand what I have seen. I understand that she is sleeping with him and that Mom doesn't know. I under-stand that it has been going on for a long time. I under-stand that my father is a person I have never looked at, capable of unimagined acts and secret obscenities. I understand. . . . I can't stop trembling and hold onto my knee, trying to stop this vibration that is shaking my body. I feel my dinner coming into my throat and dozens of images are racing through my mind: Leo kissing Mom at the breakfast table, taking me to the dentist last week, buttoning the back of Mom's dress, coming out of the shower with a towel around his middle. . . . I go into my bathroom and try to vomit, but can't, so I kneel by the toilet and put my forehead on the bowl. Marty Brooks has told me that men who sleep with prostitutes get a terrible disease. Anne Fleming must be a prostitute. My father has this disease and yet he sleeps in the same bed with my mother. I see his body, naked and diseased, and remember every dirty book I have ever read, and feel . . .

This is where the film snaps—because I have never understood what I felt at that moment. The moment when I got sick. It must have been the disillusionment, the shock. . . . No! The truth is deeper than that, and you've never wanted to face it. Why not? Why not face *everything?* It was one thing to commit your own little crimes in your own little room, but when *he* joined the ball game the world caved in. No one was pure anymore. Not parents or rabbis or teachers or the Lord himself. The whole damn world was dirty and you had never known it before! All those books Marty had given you were true: this was a revolting act, done on the sly, and something to be ashamed of. . . . (She put her white blouse on a chair and sat down beside me on the bed. And I was cold as ice because I knew it wouldn't work. Had never worked in the past and wouldn't work now. I didn't know whether to laugh or cry, because she was holding my hand and smiling at me as though it were already accomplished. No last name, just Maggie, but beautiful with long hair spilling down her back and eyes like bright jade. All I could feel was that we were two kids playing a game: you be the mother and I'll be the father and then we'll pretend to. . . . She waited for me to make a move, and when I didn't kissed me. You be the mother and I'll be the father. . . . Then I heard my own voice screaming in my head, telling me to stop before it was too late. Tell her now! But there were no words to tell such a thing, so I lay down beside her and kissed her without feeling and closed my eyes.)

The next three days were a nightmare. Every time Dad spoke to me or touched me I wanted to be sick. Mom kept asking me what was wrong, but I was alone in this thing and couldn't tell anyone. I'll run away. Leave a note saying what I saw and run away. I don't love him anymore and I wish he were dead. I can't stay here, I'll run away. And I'll never get married as long as I live, or. . . . Even Marty began to ask what was wrong, but I couldn't confide in him. There was no one to confide in. And suddenly I saw what my life was going to be. Years and years of living in this apartment with them. Years and endless years of going to school and pretending to be the same, when I was changed forever. With the sad fantastic incongruous mind of a child, I had it all figured out: my father was a sex maniac. He had a perfectly good wife, yet he had gone out and found this . . . prostitute and hired her to work for him. Buried feelings for Mom came to the surface now—love, pity, protectiveness—and every time I looked at her I could picture Leo and Anne making fun of her. Her dresses, her hair, her sad face. . . . At last it occurred to me: Benjamin.

I phoned the Jewish Library and said that I had to see him right away. "What's the matter?" he asked. Uncle

Benjamin, I can't tell you on the phone, but please please meet me on 82nd and Broadway at four o'clock. . . . I got there twenty minutes early and waited outside the snack bar. Finally I saw him wandering down the street in his usual manner—his eyes on the sidewalk, his face abstracted—and for a moment I felt like crying, because even though it was spring he was wearing his plaid muffler. I ran up and kissed him and he kissed me back. Then we crossed over to West End Avenue and started to walk uptown. "You look terrible, Davy. Is anything wrong?" I didn't speak because I knew I couldn't tell him until the setting was right. It had to be the right place and the right moment. I asked if we could walk by the river, and he nodded. Into the park on 84th Street and onto the promenade, swept with wind and sunlight. The river below.

You were so patient that day, Benjamin . . . didn't question me further, just put your arm around my shoulder while we walked. Your face was peaceful, and with your aristocratic nose and gray hair you might have been an actor—some proud and forgotten person who had once been famous for Shakespeare. Ahead of us a man with a little girl was flying a kite, two dogs running behind them. Tugboats were gliding by pushing coal barges, and big clouds were sweeping the Palisades. I kept looking at you, wondering when the moment would come, the moment when I would have to reveal that your brother had committed a crime. . . . You stopped and sat down on a bench. "I'm getting old. Can't walk without panting." I sat beside you wanting to say, No, no, you are the only person in the world who won't get old, because you belong to me and have never committed a crime in your life. Because you are perfectly good. . . . An ice cream man passed us, and you glanced at me wondering if I wanted some. I shook my head. Then I knew I couldn't wait any longer, so I let the words spill out. Uncle Ben, something has happened and I have to tell you. Maybe it'll make you mad at me, but I have to tell you anyway. It's about Dad. . . . You sighed. "Davy, you are always coming to me with stories about Leo. I know that he's hard on you sometimes, but . . ." No, I said, it isn't like that at all. It's something worse. "Your grades? Well, perhaps he's a little strict about the Math, but try to remember . . ." I grabbed your hand. You don't understand! It's something terrible! Something he's done with a woman!

A blank look came over your face—and for no reason at all you took out your pocket handkerchief, stared at it, and put it away again. The oddest look . . . like a man who had just remembered an appointment. Then I saw what was coming. Couldn't believe it, but saw it. Because, Benjamin, you whom I loved better than anyone on earth, who were sacred to me and the only person I could trust, *didn't want to hear*. It was written all over you. In your eyes that kept glancing at the river. In your fingers, toying with a pencil. In your smile that was suddenly vague. You knew what I was going to say and didn't want to hear it! Didn't want your peace disturbed, nor your loyalties split, nor your mind invaded by ugliness, nor your composure shattered by a knowledge you couldn't accept. And then—as though the veering green Hudson River sky had opened to pour light upon you—I saw you as you were. Not as I had invented you, but as you had been all along: a man who didn't want to publish a book because that would mean competition. Who didn't want to earn money because that would mean responsibility. Who loved God because the love of God was safe. Who pretended to be holy and pure and incorruptible because . . . *he was afraid of life.* You were stripped naked before my eyes in one second—and in that second my love for you died.

You spoke and I could have predicted every word, because everything that was happening seemed to have happened before, in a life that I was living for the second time.

Davy, you're probably imagining something about your father that isn't true. At your age, people imagine all sorts of things. Why don't you just put it out of your mind? You're very critical of Leo these days and I think it hurts his feelings. Now, if I were you . . .

Wind and sunlight. The wind whipping your muffler and sunlight casting silver on the waves. Dogs barking. A red kite. And oh God, please let me get away from here before I start crying again. I'm thirteen and a half, and I cry all the time . . .

Mom just called, a note of tragedy in her voice. What's the matter? I asked. What's happened? "Nothing has happened, Davy, it's just . . ." Tragic pause, me waiting patiently on the other end. "Just that I don't know what to do with myself now that your father's gone.

(*53*)

The evenings seem so long." Why don't you watch TV? I said, being of course completely insensitive to her problem, yet aware that TV wasn't a bad idea. I mean, what did they do evenings when he was alive? Read the papers, watch television, and exchange no more than two words. He would sprawl on the couch with a blank look on his face and a pile of newspapers on the floor. And there they would sit night after night without speaking, the TV going while Bessie did the dishes, and the rest of the apartment so silent it seemed to breathe. None of the rooms lived in, just the den with its stereo-FM-radio-color-television taking up one wall, and two strangers sitting in the darkness watching situation comedies without comedy or situations. After the late news and weather he would yawn loudly, go into the bedroom, undress and fall asleep. A marvelous companion. But there is little irony in my mother's temperament, so she said, "Well, maybe I will watch something. Bessie says there's an old Clark Gable movie on." I bade her good-night and returned to my empty life: no television, vacuum cleaner, roto-broiler, Waring blender, or refrigerator that makes its own ice cubes and closes its own door. I am a pauper.

Can't remember much after that day with Benjamin. . . . I guess things just returned to normal. Sure they did. In a few months I was laughing and going to movies with Marty and playing baseball. And if I had changed, no one knew it. I assimilated my father's infidelity as one assimilates a tiny dose of arsenic, and after a while Leo didn't seem so horrible to me. Or so corrupt. Funny, the way human beings protect themselves. An emotional scab had begun to form. . . . One night at dinner Leo mentioned casually that Anne Fleming had joined a firm in Chicago and moved away. So their affair was ended and my father had returned to the fold. No matter that he would do it again—that in two years I would find a letter in his pocket (while looking for spare change) from a woman who called herself "J.R." and who declared that she could not live without him. She was probably under thirty too. He liked them young, ignorant, vulnerable. . . . What did they see in him? He was fat and he was coarse, and his whole idea of sex was simple gratification. Anything beyond that would have made him uneasy—but the hypocrisy of it was fairly staggering. Making me feel dirty while he played around with young girls.

I survived . . . grew up, became twisted, and survived . . . yet everything that happened later stemmed from Leo and Anne Fleming. Every blind date that turned into a marathon of silence, every class party that cut out my heart with its close dancing couples, every opportunity for sex either ignored or gone wrong. Not one girl would do: either pretty and dumb, or ugly and smart. Either more intellectual than I was, or not intellectual enough. I had a million excuses and only Rick knew they were false. I don't like them tall. I only like them blonde. I can't stand the ones who talk too much, the ones who wear pounds of makeup, the ones who greet you at the door in hair rollers. I like them quiet, but *she* is too quiet. No, I don't want any more blind dates. For God's sake, leave me alone can't you? I have to work, study, finish this painting, go to art class, the museum, the movies, anywhere. . . . Bull sessions at Marty's, Coke and cigarettes, and six boys with one thing on their minds. Who among the dull safe older generation can ever imagine what teen-age boys talk about? Boys who but a few years ago were cute little things with lollipops and teddy bears, who loved their fathers and were tucked into bed by their mothers. . . . Revolting discussions of sex, parts of the female body described like bits of machinery, how they functioned, what they did, how they could be used. Unbelievably graphic stories of who did what to which girl, and how it was carried off, and how the girl reacted. And if one had tricked her, wonderful! Used her meanly, great! All female persons justified objects of unbridled male lust. Love? Are you kidding, man? Lists of girls drawn up by Marty, our Secretary of Sex, whole charts of which girls would and which girls wouldn't and which girls might. Girls listed and categorized as to size and shape, color and form. Discussed like livestock, really, our shouts of laughter echoing behind Marty's closed door, making his mother wonder: Now what can those boys be up to? And I, perpetual coward and non-captain of my fate, pretending to laugh with the rest. . . .

(I lay down beside her and kissed her without feeling—knowing that I couldn't say the words but that she would find out anyway. And never in my life had I felt so alone. But she surprised me, because she stopped kissing and looked up at me, holding my face in her hands. No one had ever looked at me so simply, or deeply, and I was afraid. Because whatever she wanted, I could not give it —and I was alone. "Let's go to sleep," she said. Are you sure? I mumbled, wanting to believe her, wanting so badly. . . . "Yes, I'm sure. Put your arms around me." A sigh came out of me as though I had been in mortal danger, a sigh so deep and relieved that she smiled. And curled down in my arms, and lay her head on my shoulder. "Go to sleep, David." Not Davy, but David—a new sound in my ears—and now truly and deeply asleep, all at once like a child, dark hair spilling over her face and one hand holding mine. So I slept too, and slept well for the first time in months, the thin lithe form of her fitting my arms and the little bed large enough for us both. Slept. And dreamed of a field of white lilacs and a green sea flowing beyond. Black sand and a field of white lilacs, not growing on trees but scattered somehow, making paths to the sea. . . . And woke then at dawn, rested and peaceful, no surprise finding her in my arms. No surprise, just knowing that it was all right now, because I had slept, and she was still sleeping, and had asked me for nothing. "I'm awake," she said quietly—and turning to me, brought me home.)

I JUST HAD AN INTERESTING THOUGHT. God must be a
dropout. I mean, what other reason could there be
for his sudden departure? Years and years of his
presence and then . . . nothing. A void. The more I
think about this the more I believe it. God has turned on,
tuned in, and dropped out. Just like me. The only difference is that God doesn't have relatives like mine. It's incredible, the way they keep bugging me. Mom phones and
is lonely again. Ben phones, saying be kinder to Mom.
Even Bessie calls, asking why I'm not nicer to my family.
Then the phone rings and it's Dad's lawyer wanting me to

sign papers. As if I would ever take a penny of Leo's cash.
. . . Very clever. He leaves me an income to commence
when I'm twenty-one—assuming that I will have shaped
up by then, gone back to the rat race. "People must live
in accordance with society," he used to say. So when
David is twenty-one he will be society's child. He will get
a good job, cut his hair, give up his decadent girl friend
and be good to his mother. Simplicity itself. Pluck out
your eyes and I will give you many thousands of dollars.

Which society shall I live in accordance with, Leo?
The one that murdered Martin Luther King? The one
that cracks open the skulls of demonstrators? Or maybe
the one that jails eighteen-year-olds for refusing to
slaughter on the battlefield. Useless to tell you that Man is
a society unto himself, a nation without boundaries. You
just wouldn't understand. . . . The comical thing is that
I thought you might, that I spent my entire adolescence
explaining myself to you: who I was, what I thought,
what I stood for. Every discussion ended the same way—
you slamming the bedroom door and me standing there
in tears. Mom always took your side, even when you were
wrong, and I began to feel that in some strange way I was
fighting for my life. Not my old life, but a part of me that
was just emerging.

People *aren't* inferior because of race, Dad. That
whole theory has been disproved.

OK, mister scientist, so explain to me why the colored live like they do.

Because they haven't been given opportunities.

Opportunities? What opportunities did I have?

Didn't even go to high school.

But that's different!

Listen—I was poor, your uncle was poor, and we got ahead in the world. But these people—give them a nice home, they make it dirty. Offer them a job, they throw it in your face. Why should they work? The Welfare Department supports them.

That just isn't true! We kept them in ghettos for years.

Don't talk to *me* about ghettos. I know more about ghettos than all the colored put together. A man wants to work, he can find a job. And keeping clean don't cost a penny. Even animals are clean.

Two days later it happens again. I bring up Red China, and you tell me we should drop the bomb on them. I mention the United Nations, and you go into a long speech about how it should be abolished. I learn about Medicare in my Current Events class, and you start shouting about the welfare state and those socialistic Democrats. Then one day there is . . . pot.

What are you talking about? You've used this stuff, this marijuana? You speak from experience?

Of course not, Dad. But they say it's no stronger than alcohol.

Who says? From where do you get your information? You have any idea what drugs can do to people, how they can injure the mind? For God's sake, grow up and stop giving me this nonsense. You talk like a child.

But you're not being fair. You yourself take a drink every night. More than one drink. And Mom uses sleeping pills.

That's completely irrelevant.

It isn't! You're not being fair. . . .

You swatted me away like an insect, yet I kept coming back for more. Deep inside myself I knew that I could never change your narrow bigoted mind, but I wanted acceptance. To be listened to, treated like an adult. I didn't need love from you any longer but respect, some indication that I mattered in this world. . . . The sad thing is that not once did it occur to me to walk out on you. I obeyed you like a little dog, and if I came in after curfew at night I actually trembled. I was skinny now. Still too small for my age but better looking, with thick hair that I spent hours combing and large dark eyes that I secretly thought were romantic. Things were easier at school, and in my junior year I was made president of the Arts and Letters Club. More friends, a few girls (very few), and My Work. I always thought of it in capital letters. What am I trying to find here? On the surface things weren't too bad, but underneath there were rumblings . . . like the beginning of an earthquake.

Can't seem to write anything about Mom. Maybe it's because she wasn't important to me in those days. She had changed—more chic, more stylish, busy with charity work and committees—but it was still like having a ghost in the house. When you came right down to it she didn't exist. Erased by Dad, his silent dutiful servant. And whenever a crisis occurred she would get a headache. "It's change of life," Leo told me, as though letting me in on a big secret, but this change of life never ended. Migraines, doctors' bills, the medicine chest filled with bottles. Dad had bought Shulman out of the business by now, had taken a bigger showroom and was Very Successful. But the odd thing is that these people were becoming . . . a threat to me. I lived with them, ate with them, went shopping and to the movies with them—but in disguise. Alone in my room, reading or working at the easel, I was a different person. Related to no one and aware that if only a lever could be pulled, or a secret key punched, I would come into my own. I was studying Zen. Reading Rilke in German. Working in oil and writing poetry and in love with just one person. Tchelitchew. It had hit me like lightning: wandering through the Modern Museum one day, every picture in the permanent collection known to me (or so I thought) and then coming upon *Hide and Seek*. I saw it, stopped in my tracks, and stood there for hours. Wondering how any artist, any man, could have painted my life. It was all there—a dark tree sprouting with dozens of unborn children, and a low scream seeming to echo from the canvas. A huge tree with the veined and flowered faces of children growing among the leaves, the mouths open and amazed. Hiding, yet wanting to be found. . . .

I ran upstairs to the Museum Library and found every book ever published on Pavel Tchelitchew. Gone were the abstract expressionists, the hard edge painters, the New Realists and old loves of my childhood: Redon and Balthus, Picasso and Ben Shahn. Gone, in fact, the whole long history of art. I threw away everything I was working on, bought fresh canvas and started over. The secret lever had almost been pulled because I knew what I wanted to paint now: dreams and nightmares, the locked rooms of childhood. Dancers. I had always wanted to paint circuses and was suddenly able to . . . the hopeless mechanical quality of the animals, the dirty and somehow ragged aspect of the performers, covered with grease paint and spangles. Outward glitter and inner despair. No matter that I was imitating Mr. Tchelitchew. No matter that I had become the world's greatest third-rate visionary. I *thought* I had arrived. Pavel Tchelitchew! Great genius plagued by diseases. Sensuous mystic painting his dreams. Mad paranoid looking for symbols. Tchelitchew! Saint of the canvas, able to transform his soul into gleam and glint, color and darkness . . . Then I discovered that the circus wasn't it. Nor childhood, nor dreams. What I really wanted to do was weave my poems into the paintings (had seen this done somewhere, of course). Go Tchelitchew one better and put actual words in the picture. Fortunately, I had a vast collection to draw on—one hundred unpublished and very bad poems. Well, maybe not so bad.

The Dancer

Like an animal she gazes into herself.

With the hands of the blind
She weaves the world into a garland
And becomes a world.

Her eyes, blank with knowledge,
Absorb all space, so that she moves
But to reveal its presence.

(*63*)

The startled turn, the lift, the fall,
These moments of death reveal her
As an angel glancing back.

Her small hands curve to stop my crying
When like a flower she is opened to the world
Where silence waits.

Then hot stars cease to turn.

Funny, the way I was hung-up on dancers. Had a crush on one in Martha Graham's company. She must have been the subject of that poem. . . . Then I fused poem and painting—my greatest creation—and Dad saw it. The expression on his face was almost comical, wanting to say something intelligent. "Oh. Well, now. A dancer, huh? Sure, I can tell it's a dancer. A ballet girl. But what's all the writing?" By the time I was sixteen I didn't know which was worse, his friendliness or his hostility. He was completely split, giving me money for art supplies one day, telling me to stop all this nonsense the next. Going grudgingly to a gallery with me, then getting bored and stomping out. Only Ben knew what I was trying to do, but of course he didn't offer any criticism. Just said that the pictures were very good. Ben's whole life summed up in two words. Very . . . good.

When did the battle start? The war that was to split us down the middle, leaving two armed camps. It must have been . . . no, the meeting with Rick came later. It was, I think, the day that Leo read my diary. He had stayed home from the office, had the flu or something, and when I came in around four o'clock I sensed that he was in my room. Knew it. Could almost smell it. I ran down the hall and sure enough there he was: sitting on my bed in his bathrobe, reading the most private and intimate and personal object I owned. I never dreamed that he would do such a thing, had never done it before, never went through my possessions. . . . Dad, for God's sake! What are you doing? He raised his face to me, a face so hurt and bewildered that I might have pitied him, had I not known that the whole thing was an act. "What am I doing? What are *you* doing, that's what I want to know. I wouldn't have believed it. My own son." That's none of your business! I cried. You had no right . . . "Don't talk to me about rights, mister! This is my house and I pay the rent. I wouldn't have believed it, the *filth* that's written here. What's the matter with you? Have you become a degenerate or something? Words I wouldn't use in a men's locker room. Descriptions of things. . . . You need a psychiatrist, buddy, because what I've read here is sickening. You think I've been tough on you in the past? Well, the program's just starting."

And what had he read to cause such insane revulsion? Such moral outrage? A simple, lyrical, and very beautiful description of the act of love as I imagined it to be.

From that day on I hid things. Any poem, notebook or painting that was personal. Any letter from Marty that mentioned sex. Any message to myself that spoke of my dreams for the future. (Just as I hid a doll in the closet eight years ago. But a different person then, a different human being. I am myself but in stages: busy and laughing at five, shy and sensitive at nine, at thirteen a mental case. All me, but like the leaves of an artichoke being

(*65*)

peeled away until I reach the center and find . . . what?) Two days later Dad knocked on my door, came in and sat down. The model of kindness. "Davy, I don't like what's happening to you these days. Spending so much time in here alone. You're a young boy, you should go out with other young people." I'm not lonely, I said. I have friends. "Well, sure, I know that you see a lot of Marty. But I feel you should be widening your horizons, meeting new kinds of people . . ." My heart began to sink because I knew something awful was coming. I'm fine, I said. Honest. "No, *shaifeleh,* you're not fine. Sometimes I don't even recognize you. So serious, so depressed. Look—here's what I've done. You know that country club in Westchester that the Lowensteins belong to? That nice place where we went swimming last summer? I've decided we should join." I looked at him in amazement, visions of squash courts and swimming pools rising before me. A manicured golf course, Cadillacs, and fat Jewish girls in bikinis. . . . You must be kidding, Dad. "Who's kidding? I sent the application in today." But Dad, I don't want to join a country club. He gave me a sharp look. "You're too good for such a place? Too intellectual?" I didn't say that. I mean, it would be nice for you and Mom, but why would *I* want to . . . "OK, fine! I try to do something for you, and this is what I get. A lonely boy, his father tries to help him, and this is the result. OK, stay in your room for the rest of your life. Become a hermit!"

My world threatened . . . little things . . . like him going shopping with me instead of Mom and picking out my clothes. Giving me a surprise birthday party with a group of his friends' kids: the cream of the nouveau riche. Phoning Marty and asking him to get me dates. Knocking on my door night after night . . . Mom backed him up in everything. "Your father's right, Davy. You should spend more time with young people. He's worried about you." Worried, hell. All that had happened was that he had taken a look at me. Sixteen years old and I wrote poems and painted pictures, sat in my room reading, went to art films and museums, listened to Mozart. And all of it was a threat.

Now I see it. *We threatened each other.* Like two animals sniffing around each other's territory, braced for a snarling scuffling battle. His world of money and objects and conservatism was a cannon being loaded against me, while my world made him feel . . . I don't know. A million kids in America defying their parents and running away from home, freaking-out on sex and blowing their minds on dope—while all I did was sit in my room. Because—and this is the part that hurts—I was *a very good boy.* Perfect, almost. Never missing a day of school, never criticizing my parents, well-spoken, good manners, dutiful in all things, and still thinking that there was a God up there, swimming around in a sea of mysterious stars, to whom I was responsible. Believing, actually believing, that a child should obey its parents, conform to society and acquire wealth. In some sad foggy way I had it all figured out: I would go to college, spend four useless years there, let Leo bribe some Congressman to keep me out of the army, enter his business—and paint at night. So pathetic when you write it down, but that was my plan. I would be David Marks businessman during the

day and the heir of Tchelitchew at night. And then someday when Leo was dead, I would go quietly off to Europe
and live my own life. Having paid my debt to society and
entitled to a little joy. What's odd is that I wasn't miserable about it. It was just my fate, decreed by powers over
which I had no control.

And then I met Rick.

(How to tell this without pain . . . don't know,
don't know . . . maybe it'll hurt forever. He's beyond
happiness or grief, a handful of ashes, and I helped to kill
him. Maggie can't understand my part in it, but I keep
waking at night seeing him crash to earth. . . . No matter where I go, I think of him. No matter what I read.
Some college has a demonstration, S.D.S. kids storm the
walls, and I think of what he'd have said. Black studies,
institutions crumbling at last, the whole fabric of society
changing as he wanted it to change, and him gone. A
handful of ashes. . . . Look at him now. One last look.
Because if you ever live to be old, and someone asks what
it was that saved your life and rescued you from darkness,
you'll have to answer with one word. Rick.)

My senior year. Editor of the Yearbook and an application in at Dartmouth. Decent grades, and to all in-
tents and purposes a very normal prep-school kid. A
secret artist perhaps, a part-time poet, but these things
known to few. Senior year. Excitement about who is going to which college and who is dating which girl. A few
experiments with pot, but no scandals. The Headmaster
talking to us about our futures. . . . Into this world
walks a boy named Richard Heaton the third, and all I
know about him is that he has transferred from some very

exclusive school in New England. Transferred in his last year to a strange place with dozens of strange kids looking him over. A tall blond kid who is older than the rest of us, who has a rather interesting face and smiles a lot. Who lives on Park Avenue and whose father has a seat on the Stock Exchange. And that's all. Nothing too different about him, and what the hell, I'm too busy to make new friends. We take the same classes, and the first time I really notice him is when he gets up in English and makes a speech about Thoreau and civil disobedience. Quite a speech, with tremendous knowledge behind it. Next day he speaks up in History, saying that Asia should be allowed to go Communist without U.S. intervention, and the teacher is shocked. I look at Rick Heaton and he smiles. At lunchtime we sit together.

"Boy, did you rattle him," I say. "I've never seen Mr. Foster like that."

"I didn't realize he was so conservative," says Rick.

"Conservative? His favorite president is Calvin Coolidge." We start to laugh. "How come you know so much about Communism?"

"I'm a Russian spy. . . . Your name's David, isn't it?"

"Yes. You want part of this cake?"

"No thanks. Listen, David, why are you angry all the time?"

"Angry? How do you mean?"

"I've been watching you for days, and you walk around with this terrible anger inside you."

I look at him in amazement. "Does it show?"

"To me—yes."

"Well . . . why should you care if I'm angry or not?"

"Because I like you."

No embarrassment, no evasions, just this open face looking into mine. . . . Suddenly I start talking as though I had known this kid for years, and when the bell rings neither of us hear it. We meet again after school, walk over to Central Park and talk for hours, my excitement mounting. Richard Heaton the third also wants to be an artist and is the most interesting guy I have ever met. The opposite of me—blond, upper-class, smart—yet the same inside. Parents who don't understand him, and hours spent alone painting. He has lived in Europe and bummed around Mexico. Is *not* a virgin and is telling the truth about it. Is not hung-up in the way I am, but the same inside. This is all I can think of: we are the same.

It begins to get dark, a September sky streaked with amber, and still we keep talking. Sitting by the sailboat pond trailing our hands in the water. Nursemaids take the little kids away with their boats, and soon the park is empty of all but us. We have covered our whole lives in these hours and I feel that I know him better than Marty. Better than Ben. Better than . . . myself. He asks what books I am reading, and when I tell him Proust, Gide, Flaubert, he smiles. "I'll bring you some books tomorrow. OK?" I nod and we part, each to go separately west and east. He turns back. "Hey! What's your phone number?" I call it to him and he stands there as though memorizing it, waves, and is gone. I walk home dazed.

I get to school early the next morning, telling myself that I need to study for the History test, but knowing that

I want to see Rick. He comes early too, staggering under an armful of books. Did you bring your whole library? I ask. "Sure. Why not?" The books he has brought me are books I have never heard of. Novels by Camus, Lowry and Hesse. Poems by a man named Neruda. Stringfellow's *Dissenter In A Great Society,* Brown's *Manchild In The Promised Land,* Fallico's *Art And Existentialism,* and Goodman's *Growing Up Absurd.* For a moment I am scared because this stuff seems very difficult, but he says, "You don't have to read them all. Try the Neruda first. I'd like to know what you think." I spend all day reading Pablo Neruda behind my schoolbooks. Fantastic poet. Best I have ever read. Poems like paintings, swimming with color and light. . . . Then it is three o'clock again, and without a word Rick and I head for the park.

"He's fantastic," I say. "Really beautiful. I never heard of him before."

"His work isn't very well known here," says Rick.

"Neruda—is that a Spanish name?"

"No, Chilean. He was active during the Spanish Civil War, though."

"You read a lot of poetry?"

"Sure, don't you?"

"Yes . . . I even write some. But it's pretty bad."

"Why do you keep saying things like that?"

"Like what?"

"Oh, that you write but it isn't good. That you paint but don't have much talent. You give a funny impression of yourself."

"I do?"

"Sure. I mean, I get the feeling that you know

(71)

you're good at things but don't want to admit it. Like you're afraid of getting slapped down."

"Well . . . I guess I am afraid."

"How come?"

"My father. I told you what he's like."

"That's a cop-out. If you met my father, you'd meet the same kind of person. Only not as vocal. Why do you care what they think?"

I stare at him. "You know something? I don't know."

"Can I read your poetry sometime?"

"All right. It's sort of personal, though."

He smiles at me. "So is everything."

This sudden closeness . . . dizzying, happy . . . and the end of a loneliness so deep I hadn't known it was there. A new awareness of life, as though my eyes had been splashed with cold water. An onrush of ideas. I don't know why he admired me, but I know why I did him—because he was pure. For years I had believed in things without taking action on them. But Rick lived existentially, making choices. A peace-marcher and freedom-fighter, a guy who picketed Dow Chemical and got his skull busted by the cops. Who had fasted with Quakers in Times Square and marched with black men to Washington. Who was afraid of nothing.

And why hadn't his very proper parents protested these very revolutionary activities? Because they didn't care.

That was the part that got me—their indifference. Having come from a home where my slightest sneeze was a cause of concern, I was amazed to meet Rick's family:

an effete father who drank too much and spent his life reading the *Wall Street Journal,* and a stunningly beautiful mother who did nothing but shop for clothes and antiques. Their world was made up of paintings and rare books, trips to Europe and expensive resorts, so that Rick had been raised by nursemaids and private schools. Ignored at fifteen, he had slept with an older girl while his parents were on a cruise. Alone for the summer at sixteen, he had gone to Mexico City to join the hippie culture and learn about drugs. A lonely serious kid who had grown up too soon. . . . Then I realized the secret to his parents. Rick was an A-student and had been accepted at Harvard, his father's alma mater. The outward conventions would be observed.

It was weeks before I brought him home to supper. I had been to his apartment four times, yet hadn't asked him to mine. Not because I was ashamed of it, but because . . . I was afraid. I had mentioned his name so often that Mom wanted to meet him. But Leo's reaction was typical. "Who is this character? A movie star? What's the big deal?" Having bugged me for years to make friends, Dad was now resentful. As he had been of Ben. As he would someday be of Maggie. So I delayed and delayed—because in some disastrously accurate way I knew that he would hate Rick. And I was right.

Rick arrived that evening in levis, a sweater—and sandals. His hair was even longer than usual and he had brought me some books by Céline. Leo shook hands with him, disappeared into the bedroom, and as I led Rick to my room I could hear him talking to Mom. "Who *is* this character? A beatnik or something? Wait'll you see the hair." I kept Rick in my room till dinnertime and then we all sat down at the table. Leo was eyeing him as though he were a giraffe, and as soon as soup was served he began the interrogation. "So, young man, Davy tells me you're in his class. A brilliant student. Are you going to college?" Well, said Rick slowly, I've been accepted at Harvard. . . . For a second, Dad was impressed. "Harvard, huh? I wish this kid of mine could say the same. He'll be lucky if he makes Dartmouth." Yes sir, said Rick. But you see, I don't think I'll go.

Not go? What are you talking about?

I don't really believe in college. It's more a status symbol than anything else—and I want to paint.

Paint? Paint what?

Pictures, sir. I want to be an artist.

Incredible! Accepted at Harvard and he doesn't want to go. I don't understand young people these days. What about the draft if you don't go to college?

I'm a pacifist, sir. I've applied as a C.O.

That's when Leo started to get red. His face ripened like a tomato.

Do I hear you correctly, young man?

Yes sir, I think so.

You won't fight in Vietnam?

No sir.

Well, let me tell you something. I don't know what your reasons are, but . . .

My reasons are moral, sir.

But I do know that being a draft-dodger is serious business. You think you'll ever get a job with *that* on your record?

I don't intend to get a job. I intend to paint.

The look on Leo's face was priceless. Rick's tone was so polite that it was taking all his ammunition away, and he didn't know how to proceed. No matter that he planned to keep *me* out of the army as long as possible. No matter that I had heard him tell Mom that this Vietnam thing was a mistake. For the moment he was more militant than the American Legion, and by the time dessert came he had left the table in disgust.

Rick and I listened to records for the rest of the evening, but the minute he left Dad called me into the den. I walked down the hall like someone going to the electric chair and found him sitting on the couch, all prepared. His tone surprised me though. "Sit down, Davy. No homework tonight, huh? Well, that's OK. You need a night off occasionally. So—quite a character, this friend of yours. Where did you find him?" I stared at the blank television screen. I told you, Dad, he's in my class. "Really? I didn't know they took kids like that in your school." Then my anger flared up. What do you mean, 'kids like that'? He's a very fine person! "Sure, sure. A beatnik and a draft-dodger. Very fine." He lives on Park Avenue and his father's on the Stock Exchange! I said, wishing immediately that I hadn't. "Look," said Leo, all kindness, "you know that I want you to make friends, but this character . . . well, he's not quite what I had in mind. A bit too radical for me. But if you like him . . ."

Five minutes of concerned fatherly crap and it was over. But I was relieved, because it seemed that Dad was going to let this one alone. Let it alone? He was simply waiting for the kill.

October, and the park is swept with gold . . . a warm sweet dust of Indian Summer that changes to frosty coolness at night. October, sports and classes, and Rick and I sitting by the sailboat pond, walking by the river, going to museums, films, galleries—and talking on the phone. I have seen his paintings (huge abstract canvases exploding with color) yet haven't shown him mine. He asks why. "Because they're not good enough, Rick. Wait till I do something I like." He presses the matter, so I take him home one afternoon and bring some paintings out of the closet. They are terrible, I see that now, and I stand there with my heart sinking. "Awful, huh?" He doesn't speak, taking each picture to the window and examining it: the circuses, the children, the dancer, the portrait of Ben. Then he turns to me. "You're going to be a fine painter someday—the minute you stop imitating people." My heart soars and drops, soars again. How do you mean? I ask. "These pictures show terrific skill, but you're copying someone in all of them. Tchelitchew, I think." I am amazed and baffled, and only now, for the first time, do I see what I have done . . . "People always imitate in the beginning, but you're way beyond that. Your technique is so good that you have to start over—do *your* thing and no one else's. I like the way you use the paint, but you're all hung-up with convention. I mean, I don't want to hurt your feelings, but . . ."

I knew what he meant before he finished the sentence . . . revelation, the flash of truth, insight . . . *I had to find my own style.* "You shouldn't paint what you see, but what you are," Rick said. And so I found . . . myself. Not the whole self, but a seed. A thread unravelling, my gaze turning inward. Suddenly I realized that I had been seeing with the eyes of others, forcing my vision into accepted molds, running scared. It was crazy how quickly his words affected me. . . . Within days I was painting like I had never done before, a new element coming into my work—something flat and illustrational, the colors hard. Days whirling past and sketches filling the wastebasket. Experiments with acrylic paint, money borrowed from Ben to buy paper, inks, masonite, brushes. November and the park is bare, gaunt trees against steel sky. The first snowflakes—and Rick and I run up Fifth Avenue like maniacs, catching snow in our mouths, hands, eyes. Deep snow at Thanksgiving and we build a snowman in front of school. I eat dinner twice a week at Rick's house, no longer surprised by his elegant fragile father or his mother's long speeches on Chinese porcelain. Then, just before Christmas vacation, a weird thing happens. I help Mr. Cummings move a big table in study hall, experience a sharp pain in my back and am paralyzed. Injured disc. Two months in bed, but now *draft-free.* Maimed for life unless I have a dangerous operation, which Leo won't consent to, but in two months well enough to resume school. Partially healed but never again to lift heavy objects, dive in a swimming pool or play football. What do *I* care? After college I will be free. ("No, you won't," Marty said. "They'll draft you if you can crawl.") But they didn't.

After considering a lawsuit against the school, Dad puts me to bed and hires a tutor who comes in the mornings to help me with Math and Chemistry and all the rest. I endure him (because I am flat on my back), do the minimum amount of work and wait patiently every day for 3:45. At which time my door will open, and Richard Heaton the third will come charging in with books and records and magazines. And himself. In a way, those were the best times—the long winter afternoons of coffee and records. Hours when we didn't speak, but listened to Dylan and Baez and the sad little child-songs of Donovan. Record jackets everywhere. Snow drifting past the window and the radiator clanking softly. . . . He would be stretched out on the floor humming, or just silently watching the ceiling, his clear blue eyes encompassing the world. (And your eyes are buried now in a strange land. A land I can't even imagine, with farmers sowing their fields as bombs fall and oxen dragging plows. Farmers you didn't want to kill for because you wouldn't kill for anyone—not even yourself. Blond boy whose ashes fertilize strange fields. Pacifist dying in a blazing whirling helicopter. Did you scream? I can't think of it, your dying. It is too terrible.)

Four a.m. Memories, time out of sequence, and no way to sleep. Close the mind and he comes rushing in. "Hey! Guess what I found today?" A book, a record, an ancient banjo, a 30's tie. Indian prints on Orchard Street, scrap metal on First Avenue. Scavenger in levis and sweater. Modern Odysseus roaming New York. "Guess what I found?" An old art magazine, a deck of Tarot cards, a pawnshop flute. Our endless talks . . .

(78)

"I've always been against it, Davy. I would have been against it even in Hitler's time. There are always justified wars, but the result is the same. People die."

Two wooden swings in Central Park. Swinging in the middle of winter while little kids in snowsuits stare at us.

"But what good does it do to resist? There are so few of you."

"If people keep refusing to go, the thing will become world-wide. Don't you see? Take away armies and you take away war."

"War is different now. You only have to press a button. . . ."

Swinging back and forth, the swings creaking. Patches of snow and icy wind. His cheeks red.

"Yes, but who makes the missiles? Men. And who runs the Pentagon? Men. Even the guy who presses the last button is only a man. And men can be changed by the power of example."

"I don't know. It seems impossible."

"Everything good seems impossible. Look at Jesus. Love one another, he said, and they thought he was crazy. But he changed the world. Gandhi too. And Buddha—walking into the wilderness."

"They'll call you a coward. . . ."

"I don't care. Hey! Look how high I'm going. Up up and away!"

"Be careful! You'll break the damn thing. Aren't

you afraid of what your father will say?"

"Nope."

"Well, I am."

"That's the trouble with you, Davy. You keep agreeing with them."

Higher and higher with the park below. Why can't I be like him? Higher and higher in the blue wind. Afraid of no one.

"I *don't* agree with them."

"Sure you do. Which is why you're still playing the parent-child game. Cooperating all the way. Why don't you do your own thing and see what happens?"

"Very funny."

"No, very serious. Can't you see that your life is your own? Do your own thing—and fly. Hey, this is great! I'm almost over the top."

He will leave that swing and fly into eternity. He will take a giant leap with his hair blown back. He will catapult into happiness, a silver happiness, while the dark world spins below.

And suddenly . . . I want to go too.

It began in February—a series of remarks so casual that I might have missed them had Dad's voice not had an edge to it. A series of very strange and disparate remarks that would come at any hour of the night or day. "Who brought these flowers? Rick? So what is he planning to be, a florist?" Little things: "That kid should take more sports. He's too flabby." Casual things: "He's coming over again? What's the matter with this character? No girl friends?" Then stronger: "OK, I've been patient for a long time, but I don't like what's going on. I know he comes from a good home, but there are certain things about him, certain . . . characteristics I don't like. See some other people for a change. Let Marty get you some dates."

OK, Leo, two can play this game. You want to dispose of Rick. Right? Break it up, get rid of the "hippie" influence, get me under your thumb again. Very well, I shall plan a counterattack. Because even though you have ruined everything in my life, you are not going to ruin this. I will capitulate the better to deceive you. Invite Marty and his friends over as camouflage, see Rick at his house instead of mine, and, God help me, date a million girls. Pretty girls, ugly girls, stupid girls, and girls who are so smart they frighten me. The whole freaking universe is filled with girls, and if you want me to date them I will. Just as long as this one thing—this most precious thing—is not ruined. There is Helen Donahue: fifteen, fat, and a Catholic, whose sole aim in life is to get deflowered and repent it later. Joan Wiener: who looks exactly like her name and rides in horse shows. Barby Baxter: who is "coming out" this year and calls her mother "Mummy" and talks baby talk. There is even a girl I like, a friend of Rick's named Nicole. Two years older than I and studying at the Art Students League. A tall quiet girl who doesn't care that I am younger, and who likes to go to museums. Marvelous. I bring her to the house for inspection and then we leave to meet Rick. Go to the movies, take Nicole home, and down to the Village where we browse through bookstores and buy records.

It is spring now, with cool winds and sculptured clouds, and I am accepted at Dartmouth. Rick's parents are in Greece and we have his apartment to ourselves: set up easels in the dining room and paint for hours. Fads don't bother me anymore—kinetic art, neo-concretism, assemblage, mixed media—and Tchelitchew seems Victorian. I don't *care* about other artists, not even Rick who is brilliant, because I'm involved in discovery. Negative space. Reduced perspective. Flat flat surfaces, like illustrations, the colors sharp. My work is becoming my own.

(When did I decide to leave? Can't remember . . . it must have started that day on the swing . . . the realization that my life was my own, a burning necessity to enter the stillness of myself, to find the truth of who I was. A fever. It was like I was standing on the edge of a precipice, a fantastic area of free space that was waiting for me to fill it. And Rick would help me. Would tell his parents of his letter turning down Harvard, and get a place with me in the Village. Wonderful, impractical plans: I would take a part-time job and paint. He would put in his time as a conscientious objector in some hospital and stay with me weekends. We would save money to go to London where everything was happening. We would be free. . . . The vision of it. Like light to a man who had been blind. Like air and sun to a man who had been in prison. No father twisting my life with his demands, no mother worrying and worrying, no laws and rules and hypocrisies. Just freedom—a lamp burning in rain.)

Having taken his fears underground, Leo let them emerge again, but in different ways. Stubborn, possessive, unwilling to ever let me go, he found a new topic: How I Had Changed. "It's true Davy. Even Arnie Lowenstein noticed it last night. Said how different you looked." Dad, for God's sake . . . "OK, OK, I know I'm old-fashioned, but the way you kids dress these days . . . sloppy, your hair too long. You never used to look like that. You always had a very neat appearance." Please, Dad! "I'm not supposed to mention these things? My own son dressing like a hippie, and I shouldn't mention it?" I'm *not* dressing like a hippie. "So what would you call it? Beau Brummell?"

A week of peace and then he finds another gambit. "You still seeing that hippie character? What's his name?" You know his name, Dad. Rick Heaton. "OK, Rick. You still seeing him after school?" Well sure, I see him occasionally. "I thought so. The habits you're acquiring you didn't pick up at home. Chain-smoking, sleeping late, walking around like a bum when you have a closet full of clothes. What's happening to you?"

What's happening . . . why are you different . . . why have you changed. . . . Ignorant man, can't you see that I'm growing up? Cracking the shell of my old life and poking my head out. Everything is beginning for me, and if you can't understand it, too bad. I don't belong to you anymore. I can run, I can sing, I can dance. I can be a fool or a wise man, a dunce or a clown. I can sit on a mountain and meditate, sell my poems on street corners, live in a tent. I don't belong to you, and you have no rights over me. Can't you see that? *No rights at all.* And if I ever have kids, I will let them grow like weeds and never

(*83*)

spoil the world for them. . . . Dizzying, this sense of self. Like getting drunk on air. A free trip. A sober high. I am myself and what I will be. I am strong, an artist. I am capable of love.

Then . . . the crash. Some buyers come to dinner, and after I leave the table I hear Leo talking to them in the living room. As usual he is lying about me, bragging, but tonight, as though he knew I could hear him and knew exactly what reaction it would provoke, he begins mapping my future. "Sure, sure, accepted at Dartmouth weeks ago. I'll drive him up myself, get him off on the right foot. A gorgeous campus—and a great business school. By the time he enters the firm he's gonna make his old man look dumb. (Laughter) Well listen, they learn things in school today that you and I never heard of. Everything scientific, up-to-date. A good education and then I want him to marry a nice girl, move out of the city. Westchester, maybe. Some life, huh? *We* should have had it so good."

Suddenly I start sweating—sweat pouring down my face so hard that I have to wipe it out of my eyes—and my heart is pounding. Now, only now, this night, this moment, do I understand my predicament. I have been dreaming all these weeks, thinking that things would take care of themselves, when all the while my future has been poured in concrete. I never believed it would happen, and now it is happening as surely as if we had skipped a reel in the movie of my life—jumped forward to the day when I am no one, my features erased, my talent numbed, my soul a blank. The heir of Leo Marks.

I run over to my desk, put some paper in the typewriter, and begin to write Leo a letter. . . .

I must have typed for two hours—words hitting the paper like bullets, everything misspelled—but the meaning like a cry. For the first time in seventeen years I was asking him to help me, begging him, telling him that I couldn't live the life he had planned, that I couldn't go to college or enter his business. . . . Please, I said, please try to understand. I'm not the person you've made up in your mind, I'm only me, David. I know how much you care about my future, but it has to be *my* future. Don't you see? You've arranged my whole life when all I want to do is paint. I'll go crazy if I can't be an artist, kill myself. . . . No, I don't mean that. All I want is a chance. It isn't that I'm not grateful, it's just that I want so much to be something special in this world. Remember how you used to tell me about the arguments you had with your father? How you found him old-fashioned? It's the same with us. You're one generation and I'm another, and the same values can't apply. In all these years you've never seen me as a human being, just a child, so if I'm rebelling now it isn't that I don't love you but that I have to grow up. . . . I don't know how to say this, but there are times when I feel I could be something beautiful if only I had the chance. It's like a part of the Bible we read in assembly the other day: "To every thing there is a season, and a time to every purpose under heaven. A time to be born, and a time to die . . ." Well, this is my time. My time to be born. Dad, please try to understand this—I've got to leave home. Get away from here and find out who I am. I've got it all figured out: I'll get a place of my own, and a part-time job, and paint. I know that sounds ter-

(*85*)

rible to you, but who knows? I might become a very great painter someday and make you proud. You always act like these things don't matter, art and creativity, but I can't help feeling that deep inside yourself you know that there is more to life than money and security and the rent paid. I'm saying this all wrong, but. . . .

Pages and pages of words. Talking to him more intimately than ever in my life. Every hope, every dream. And to this day, I remember the last paragraph of that letter.

I know I've left you out of things, and hurt you by it, and I'm sorry. Because it's still not too late for us to respect each other. We were close once—remember? And I always admired you so much when I was little. So please try to understand why I'm doing this. I'm grateful for everything you've given me, even if you don't think I am, and I do love you. So please forgive me. And help me.

David

LEO NEVER ANSWERED the letter. In fact he never even mentioned it. For three whole weeks I looked in the mailbox every morning, waited for him to say something at dinner, sat in my room hoping he would knock. Nothing. Just an indifference so studied and casual that I finally realized what he was doing: blocking it out. So a part of me died. Nothing dramatic about it, just one of those little griefs you never get over or forgive. Because I haven't forgiven you, Dad, and if there is a life after death I hope you are suffering there. You terrible terrible coward. Just once did I try to reach you—and

(87)

you turned away.

Dark skies that morning, and rain. You always hated rain yet you were buried under it. With fire engines wailing in the distance and a rabbi mumbling some prayers. Mom, Ben, and me—listening to the strange words and staring at the earth that was about to receive you. Funeral flowers heaped on the mud, jets from Kennedy Airport screaming overhead. All the noises of the city singing you into the ground, and the rabbi's monotonous voice, and my mother crying. I didn't cry, Leo, because even then I held that unanswered letter against you. My unanswered life. I just kept lighting a cigarette that wouldn't light, until Benjamin took it away. Then, a strange thing. Dolly Marks who hadn't shown her feelings in years—pale, inhibited woman, my mother—dropped to her knees and tried to hold onto the coffin as it went down. Groped for it, grabbed at its handles, screaming, "Leo, don't leave me! Leo!" And had to be pulled away by Benjamin as the box went into the earth. Ben and I holding her elbows, leading her up the path, mascara streaking her face. At the gate she broke away from us and tried to run back. "I can't leave him there! I can't leave him alone!" No, said Benjamin, no. Come now, Dolly, it's all right. Everything will be all right. . . . "How can I leave him there alone? In the rain? Oh my God, help me. . . ."

Even then. With my mother sobbing, and my uncle fighting to control himself, and people staring at us, and the whole crazy day tilting and veering under dark summer rain, even then . . . I felt nothing.

A monster, you called me. A person of no feelings.

Well, maybe I am. You said it so often that I came to believe it. It's true: I don't have any feelings. I'm a freak, cruel, inhuman, a sadist. No love for my parents. A golden child, loved, fed, clothed and educated. Pampered and spoiled and put to bed when he sneezes. What does he do? Runs away from home and destroys his father. ("You're destroying your father. You know that, don't you? Destroying him.") But who shot first, Leo? You or I? All I did was write a letter that never got answered.

Who . . . shot . . . first?

You. With your cowardice and hypocrisy. With your avoidance of life. With your lies and conventional cruelties, and your sense of justice that was so Very American. In a family court you would have been right. (Your teen-age son has defied you and left home? Gone to live with those, ugh, dirty hippies in the Village? Gone to smoke dope and commit fornication? Guilty! Guilty for being true to himself. Guilty for being . . . young.)

Finally it occurred to my blank little mind that you were never going to answer the letter. Never going to mention a thing I had said, but simply take me to Europe as a graduation present, and then drive me to college. (But what did I expect? I knew what he was like, knew what a hypocrite he was. *What did I expect?*) I could have had many reactions, I guess, but the only reaction I found was silence. Mute in the mornings, mute at the dinner table. Barely answering when you spoke. Not outright rebellion, but rebellion David-style. At first you ignored it. Then you tried to kid me but I wouldn't take the bait. You tried kindness, phony kindness, and I wouldn't respond. Next, a bribe—a nice little convertible for

(*89*)

college, the brochures spread out on the table—and I looked at them without speaking. At last you got mad. "OK mister, I've had enough of this. I don't know what you're trying to prove, but I'm not buying it. When I talk to you, you answer! Hear me?" I hear you very well, I said politely, and left the room. . . . All I had to do was release my anger, yet I still couldn't do it. *Why?* What is this thing in me that can never get mad? I go along with a situation until it gets so terrible that I explode. And then it's too late—people's feelings fly into the air like shrapnel. . . . Unable to protest, I lit the wick for the explosion instead. A long wick with a fizzing spark at the end, whose stages were: seeing Rick openly, playing records at top volume, smoking two packs a day, coming in after curfew, doing no homework, growing my hair and . . . ha, I forgot: getting drunk. Leo and Mom at the movies, and me in the den with a fifth of bourbon, plastered for the first time in my life. Reeling around in my bare feet as Simon and Garfunkel pound their mournful collegiate melodies. Doing a little dance and falling flat on my face. Giggling. Not the marijuana-giggle, but the square giggle of too much booze. Groovy groovy groovy. I . . . am . . . drunk.

What do I see in the doorway? Two faces like moons, and many pairs of eyes. Shocked expressions. It is my mother and my father and they have caught me. Good little David is zonked. I do not understand what they say. All I know is that (miraculously) I am stuffed into a pair of pajamas and put to bed. The golden child. . . . An hour later I wake up with a parched mouth and hear them talking next door. I feel awful.

OK, so all kids do it. But why now? What the hell's the matter with him?

Something's bothering him, Leo. He's been like this for weeks.

Bothering him? What should bother him? He lives like a king.

It isn't that, dear, it's . . .

I'll tell you what it is! It's that weirdo he's friends with. I knew I shouldn't let it continue.

But Leo . . .

A bad, disruptive influence! Probably give him drugs next. Did he ever drink before this? Did he?

I sit there with my head throbbing and say to myself: Oh, David, if you are ever going to do it, do it now. Get up and put on your clothes and leave. Please please leave. Because the next thing he will do is forbid you to see Rick. It's so easy. Just get up and put on your clothes. . . .

Paralysis. Fear. Not willing to do it overtly, but trying to force the issue in little ways. Purposely failing a History test. Coming in so late that he was frightened. Finally, being rude to him. What did I want? To infuriate him until he locked me in my room? Perfect excuse: he locks me up and I jump out the window onto the terrace below, flee in my underwear and charge Mental Cruelty. . . . It finally happened of course. Had to. A silent breakfast with Bessie serving waffles, Mom staring at her plate, and Leo suddenly (BANG) pounding the table. Out of nowhere. "OK, I've had it. You're not gonna see that character again." Who? I say, baffled, my mind on breakfast. "That hippie character, Rick. I've been soft on you, buddy, but now I'm laying down the law. I'm not gonna sit here and watch your whole personality being changed by some . . . oddball." Mom opens her mouth to speak, but he bangs the table again. "Not a word! I've had it up to here!" (David, if you are ever going to do it, do it now. Get up and put on your jacket and leave. It's so easy. Just get up and put on your jacket.) Can't. Icy fear streaking through me and the waffle cold in my mouth. It was only a dream, leaving this place. Only a sad little dream. He is stronger than you are, a puppet-master who holds all the psychological strings. *And you will never get away from him.*

Nightmares and cold sweats. The spring semester almost finished and a Cinemascopic view panning before me. Europe and college. Business Administration. Find a girl and marry her. Make babies. Become successful and alcoholic. Blow your brains out. . . . For the first time in years I pray to God. Sit in Rick's room with my head in my hands. . . .

"I can't do it, I can't. He'll kill me."

"No, he won't, Davy. You just have to approach him the right way."

"There *is* no right way. I can't even talk to him. He's like a dictator."

"You're still capitulating inside. Your position's dishonest. . . ."

"How can you say that? You haven't told your parents about Harvard, and it's *April.*"

"My mother's been in the hospital, you know that.

Look, you're making too much of this."

"I'm not! Rick, please help me. I can't do it alone."

"Well, maybe I could talk to him or something. I know he hates my guts, but maybe I could get through to him."

"You think so?"

"Sure. I mean, what crime are you committing? All you want to do is leave home. The trouble is, he can't treat you like an adult until you act like one."

"You don't know what college means to him."

"Of course I do. He's a self-made man, so education is a very big deal. Don't worry about it, Davy. I'll help."

And I . . . believed him.

How can I write this next part? I don't even know which words to use. I've never told it to anyone—Ben, Marty, Maggie—keeping it all to myself, rocking it to me like a dead child. I don't know the words because some things are beyond words, beyond feelings, a paralysis of the heart. . . . Whisper it. Sing it. Get high and dance it. Because it's the crux of everything you've written here, and the reason for the whole story. . . .

Scene: a warm night in May, my parents at a party, and Rick and I reading in my room. Defying Dad, yet planning to leave before he comes home. Time: nine o'clock. Vibrations: excellent. I am at the desk while he lies on the bed, smoking, humming, flipping pages of books. We have not spoken for an hour, but there is harmony between us tonight, a certain peace, as though we have both decided that things will work out. (These hours and minutes are painted on my mind, and I can remember the shirt he was wearing and the hole in his shoe, and the way his hair fell down hiding his eyes.) Misty night, warm spring, a few raindrops. And it seems to me that we have been friends for a hundred years, and that nothing can hurt us or happen to us because we are at peace together. No suspicions or criticisms. He accepts the squareness of me as I accept the difference of him, and for a little time, this night only, the world seems good. . . . With a sudden twist of mood he rolls off the bed and starts to laugh. Laughing for no reason at all, but infectious laughter, so that I join him. Then we are horsing around, sparring, doing an Indian war dance, everything getting sillier by the moment. He does an imitation of Chaplin, his hero, and it is very funny. I push him and he topples over. "You're too flabby!" I yell, imitating Dad. "Why don't you take more sports? What kind of all-American kid are you?" We are wrestling now, trying to see who is stronger—and panting we crash to the floor. Give up? he asks. "No!" I shout, and try to pin his arms behind him. He gets the better of me, and straddles me, forcing me down. Still we are laughing, amazed to find ourselves doing something so classically youthful. Pleased, almost, to find ourselves wrestling like two characters out of a turn-of-the-century boys' book. It occurs to me that I will probably hurt my back again, so I laugh all the harder. And his laughter is filling the room like wonderful crazy music, his yellow hair swinging over his eyes. There is a crash. The door has burst open. It is . . . I don't know. Someone has kicked open the door. It. . . . Someone is pulling Rick off me, his face contorted. Someone is. . . . Yes—Leo. But like a madman, pulling Rick off, yanking him away by the collar. But . . .

why? "OK, sonny, that's it, that's all, everything's over. Now, out! *Out of this house.*" It is happening too fast. My father is dragging Rick into the hall and his voice is murderous. He's hurting him! I run down the hall, and Leo has backed Rick up against a table, his fist clutching Rick's collar, his face white with a rage I do not understand and cannot believe. What is . . .

I can't, I just can't. Skip it. Go on. It was terrible enough when it happened, much less repeating it. Skip it.

Ten minutes later I packed a bag. This action I had prayed for was happening all by itself, without thought, without plan, without desire. Maniacally cool, I threw things into the suitcase—blazer, gray flannels, shirts, underwear, toothbrush—while Leo paced and shouted and swore. Mom stood in the doorway, unable to believe what she was seeing. But he never touched me, not once. Didn't grab me or bar the door, didn't prevent me in any way. And I know why. Because I would have killed him had he laid a finger on me. Killed him with pleasure while my mother watched. . . . I threw one book in the suitcase—Neruda—jammed it shut and marched down the hall. He came after me then, practically incoherent, listing all the things he had given me during my lifetime. Staggering down the hall with whole lists of things streaming out of his mouth: my clothes, my education, summer camp, art supplies, my membership to the Modern Museum, doctors' bills, bicycles, roller skates, season tickets for baseball. A long and amazing litany which was supposed to spin me around, drop me to my knees, and make me beg forgiveness.

(*95*)

I opened the front door and paused. Turned. Looked him in the eye. Then, with a joy I will never again be able to summon or repeat, I told him to go to hell.

In forty minutes I was at Marty's on East 12th Street, sitting in the kitchen and shaking. "What happened?" he kept asking. "What did he do to you?" I can't tell you, Marty, but I'm not going back. Not even if he sends the police. I've had it, I'm finished, I'm not going back. "But what did he *do?*" I told you. I don't want to talk about it! The phone rang. Don't answer it! I said. "I've got to, Davy. For God's sake . . . Hello? Oh, yes sir. Yes, he's here. No, he's all right. Just a little upset. No, really—he's OK. Look, Mr. Marks, why don't you let him spend the night here? No, you don't have to come down. Just let him spend the night and get cooled off. OK? Fine, fine. He'll be home tomorrow, sir. Don't worry about him."

But I didn't go home for two years . . . and by that time my home was stranger than the strangest country. A place where I didn't know the language.

Leo called every morning, talked to Marty, put on an air of great patience. But when three days had passed and I hadn't gone to school, he came down to the Village. I thought I was prepared, but when I heard that knock at the door my knees went weak. Marty was in class. No one to help me. . . . I opened the door and he entered the room slowly, mingled expressions fleeting over his face: relief that the apartment was decent, embarrassment at seeing me again, fatherly determination warring with his discomfort at having to fight this battle on strange

(*96*)

ground. He looked around and chose the wicker chair. I stood by the window, facing him.

Quite a place Marty's got here. Not bad. A rough neighborhood, though. Well. How are you feeling?

Fine.

Feeling OK?

Yes.

So now we've both cooled off, huh? Your mother's still upset, though. Cries all the time. I told her I'd bring you back this afternoon.

You must be kidding.

Who's kidding? We had a little disagreement, now it's over. Davy, I want you to come home.

Not a chance.

But . . .

I said: not a chance.

What are you trying to pull on me? You're seventeen years old.

Right. And next year I'll be eighteen.

Davy, look. These things happen between fathers and sons—arguments, disagreements. It's part of growing up. But I can't just let you stay here, miss school. . . .

Why not?

Why? Because you're a minor, a young boy.

Don't make me laugh.

(*97*)

Now look, I've had to put up with a lot from you!

Yeah, sure.

You want to have another fight? Is that what you want? Well, I'm not buying it. I want you to come home and behave like a decent human being.

And that's when something in me broke.

A decent human being? Who are *you* to talk about decency? You hypocrite! Doing that to Rick and then coming down here as though it never happened! What are people to you? Just things to use and hurt and toss around? You awful hypocrite! Trying to make everything dirty that you don't understand. Hurting people, destroying them. . . . You think I'll ever come home after what you did? You can roast in hell before I'll ever . . .

I was crying now, trembling with my own impotent rage, leaning my forehead against the window and sobbing. He came over to me.

OK, sonny. Take it easy. No one's gonna force you to come home if you don't want to. Take it easy, David. I know you're upset. You think I don't know that? It's all right, son. You come home when you're ready. OK? When you're ready.

The strangest syndrome of my life . . . going back to school, doing my homework with Rick, eating sensibly, dressing properly—but sleeping at Marty's. A pale exile. Mom phoning twice a day, Ben meeting me for lunch to find out what had happened (I wouldn't tell) and the

Headmaster finally calling me into his office—his dull voice a mixture of modern tolerance and Victorian disapproval. . . . These people who had never once wondered who I was, or what I felt, were now desperately trying to comprehend and humor me lest I—what? Kill myself? Break off family ties forever? It was really funny how everyone became so tolerant. Not once did Mom reproach me for anything, and never again did Leo come down to 12th Street. He just kept waiting and waiting, phoning Marty, phoning Ben, dropping me little notes saying how much everyone cared. Who knows? Maybe he had consulted a psychiatrist. No. The real reason was that he knew he had pushed me too far. Besides . . . he trusted Marty. Martin Brooks, friend of my childhood, whose family was Jewish and rich. Marty, who could be counted on to take care of me. Whose parents had so much faith in him that they had given him his own apartment. Who had always been admired by Leo and Mom because he was the epitome of the normal clean-cut all-around American boy.

Except that he wasn't. Which was the biggest joke of all. This staunch protector, to whom my father had entrusted me in a time of trial, was really a bum. Your phrase, Leo, but it suited him to a T. An incredible joke. Good old Marty, whom you called every day to see how I was, had become . . . how shall I put it . . . not a plastic hippie, but a *moonlight* hippie. An N.Y.U student during the day and king of the flower people at night. I don't know how it happened, because the last time I had seen Marty he had just been my square oversexed pal from West End Avenue. But these days . . . in his very own words: "Oh wow, man. Too much!"

"What kind of traveling you like?" he asked, the second week I was living with him. "I mean, what do you dig? Tea, happy dust, crystal? Some sweet little cactus buttons?" Marty, I said patiently, what is this new language you're speaking? "Language? Why, Travel Guide English, of course." Oh, come on, I said. Come off it. "Come off what? Don't you want Martin to get you some stuff? Don't you want to have a good time?"

In other words, our Marty was a dealer in dope. A great little businessman who could supply you with the best Acapulco Gold for a certain price. Or acid, if that was your thing. Or STP, if you really wanted to freak out. Or smack, if you were sick enough to need it. . . . Shall I confess something? I was shocked. The closest I had ever gotten to this world was *Life* magazine, and now I was living in it, right in the midst of Marty's entourage: strange strange kids who had names like Cowboy and Chester and Preacher, and who panhandled or dealed for a living. Guys like Valiant who made cookies laced with pot and sold them in schoolyards. Girls like Happytime who balled anyone who would give her speed. Pale sick people who lived in communal pads and caught each other's lice and washed each other's backs in a dirty communal tub. Who dressed in ponchos and bells and went barefoot in winter. Who got busted and went to jail for possession, and got sprung, and made the scene again. Who lived like paupers but had the best stereo systems in the world. Who lay around evenings on mattresses as the joint was passed from hand to hand, and the music blared, and the incense wafted from paisley wall to paisley wall. And whose parents . . . were looking for them all over America.

Hey man, that's groovy. . . . Don't hassle me, boy. . . . Oh, he burned me, he really burned me. . . . You wanna cop some acid? . . . Well, you know, they have their power-trips and ego-trips, but like, why should I interfere? . . . So I dropped this cap, and man, King Kong! . . . And there is this spade chick sitting there, rapping and rapping, when all *I* want to do is . . . Clever Martin Brooks. Making this scene every night, but always at someone *else's* pad. Keeping his own place immaculate in honor of visiting parents. Getting teeny-boppers to run the stuff for him so he could never be spotted as a connection. Playing father to little street junkies and fourteen-year-old derelicts because they put out for him, in more ways than one.

OK, so I was shocked. But also bitter. Because Rick Heaton, whom Dad blamed for my downfall, had left this scene years ago—while Marty was trying to drag me into it. Boy, did he try. Everything from free acid to a nice little orgy, but I wanted no part of it. I was still numb from what had happened and I followed Rick around like a beggar, hoping . . . Christ, I don't know what I hoped for. Our plans were still the same but there was something new between us, a fear, a reticence. . . . All I could think of was June, when we would be out of school. I even began looking at apartments for us, drumming up my courage, trying to make myself stronger, hoping . . . that he would forget. Then the phone call came.

Nine at night, Marty over at Cowboy's, and the

phone rings. I flop down on the paisley-covered bed and answer it.

"Hello?"

"Davy?"

"Yes."

"It's Dad, Davy. How are you?"

(I have not spoken to him for days, but the sound of his voice brings it all back. The hallway. Rick.)

"I'm OK."

"And Marty?"

"The same."

"Good, good. I'm glad that everything's all right. Davy, listen, I'll tell you why I'm calling. It's about your passport photo."

"My what?"

"Your passport picture. You have to have it taken this week."

"What are you talking about?"

"Our trip to Europe. All the papers are ready."

"You can't be serious."

"So all you have to do is have the picture taken. And I bought you some new luggage at . . ."

"I'm not going to Europe with you, Dad. You know that."

"At Mark Cross. Brown leather."

"Well, I'm not going."

"I bought you a camera, too . . ."

(Long pause. I light a cigarette and wait.)

"Davy?"

"Yeah, I'm here."

"How long are you going to keep this up?"

"I don't know what you're talking about."

"Don't you care about your mother at all? She cries every night. And the doctor is worried about her. Never once did she come down to Marty's or bother you. Don't you have any feelings for her?"

"Do you?"

"What did you say?"

"I asked if *you* had any feelings for her. Because you're always talking about me—while meantime you play around. Right? Play around on the side."

(It has finally come out. The last weapon in my arsenal, and one I thought I would never use.)

"What *the hell* are you . . ."

"I'm talking about Anne Fleming, and all the ones who followed her. So just forget about . . ."

"You little bum! What are you trying to pull on me? I don't even know what you're referring to!"

"Oh, yes you do."

"OK! That's it! I'm sending the cops down there. You're gonna come home this minute."

"You won't send the cops, Leo. And do you know why? You're afraid I'll tell Mom."

"I . . . I never thought you were like this, Davy. I don't even know you anymore."

"OK, now you do. Because if I have to fight dirty, I will. And if honor is bugging you, then forget it. You never *taught* me any honor. Lying, cheating, playing around—that's the only example I ever got from you."

"What are you saying to me?"

"All I ever got from you was money. And money isn't the answer! I wanted to respect you and I couldn't.

Cheating on taxes, forcing Shulman out of the business, playing around with young girls. I *wanted* to respect you . . ."

"Davy, I'm your father . . ."

"Well, that isn't enough! I didn't want just a father, I wanted some decency in the world. And you were corrupt from the beginning."

"Shut up, you! Talking about corruption while you live off my money. Who's been supporting you all these years? You didn't worry about corruption then, just took and took. Your hand out and money pouring into it. I'm not gonna phone you anymore, I swear to God."

"That'll suit me fine."

"But you'll be sorry for this! God will punish you."

"Yeah, sure. Bring God into it. Bring Moses too."

"What's *happened* to you? Have you no feelings for anyone? My own flesh and blood . . ."

But I had hung up.

Three days later I graduated . . . and as I stood on the platform I could see Mom's pale face in the audience, and Ben next to her—and Leo's empty chair. Then I had a diploma in my hand, and the three of us were heading for a restaurant to "celebrate." Except that we couldn't because of everything that had happened. We talked about it for a long time as the lunch got cold, Ben spouting platitudes—but I'll say this much, Mom tried to understand. She had witnessed the whole incident with Rick, and had been shocked by it, so that she knew I was right. I couldn't live at home anymore.

It isn't that part that worries me, Davy. It's giving up your education. Why don't you try college for a year? Just one year.

I don't want to waste the time. You know I would have gone to college if he had let me major in Art, but the way things are now . . .

But how will you live? You can't stay with Marty forever.

Rick and I will get a place together. I'll find a job.

Davy, I'm willing for you to stay with Marty for the summer because I think you'll change your mind. In the fall, when all your friends go off to school . . . well, you may feel differently then. But please make up with your father.

I can't do that, Mom.

Darling, there's no such word as can't. You don't know how he's suffering . . .

Yeah, I bet.

Why do you hate him so? The man would die for you. You're all he has in the world. Please make up with him—for me.

I promised her, even though I knew Dad and I were finished. Made this last promise because she was so sad and defeated, and because she had always been good to Rick. A few days later she brought my things down to Marty's deceptively neat apartment, and asked me to call her every week, and then . . . I was on my own.

Strange freedom. Desired for so long, and now . . . what to do with it? Go to bed when you want, get up when you want. Skip meals. Live on hot dogs. Take money from the savings account and buy books and records. Sit in Tompkins Square Park in the evenings, listening to guitar players and watching the runaway children dance in their bare feet. Headbands and donkey bells and beads. Faces painted with Day-Glo. Dogs and cats and babies and the little runaway children who sleep on park benches. Strangest freedom of all: the freedom to choose. Paint, I tell myself, study, go to galleries—and yet I do nothing. Simply wander the streets looking at faces and talking to all the kids who panhandle me. I give them a quarter and listen to their troubles, but think: I'm just like you, the bridges burned and nowhere to go. . . . This great loneliness—Rick in Newport with his parents, where he will tell them of his C.O. application—and me trying to avoid Marty's lures. "Want to come over to Cowboy's, man? Want me to get you a chick?" No. It is enough for me to wander the streets in my long hair and old chinos, looking like all the rest, but inside myself a stranger. I am living here but this is not my life, this world of crash pads and runaways, of pot and hash and blaring music. I was never attracted to it before and am not now, because it seems so . . . mindless. A cultivated mindlessness. Kids lying in doorways reading comic books, twenty-year-olds shooting marbles on the sidewalk, the touristy shops, and a million squares pouring into The Electric Circus on weekends. (Oh my. So *this* is what it's all about. Oh my goodness. How psychedelic.) Strange strange freedom which baffles me with its dullness until I realize something: it is nothing without Rick. He has only sent me one letter saying that he hasn't told them yet because of "certain complications," and being me—stupid, naive—I do not see what is happening to him. See nothing but one day turning into another and the long hours I must spend in the park because Marty has some girl in the pad. And yet I do not want a girl, and lie awake at night suffering over this. The Village is filled with them— all kinds of girls who will do all kinds of things—but I keep my distance, Leo's words that night haunting me. Marty thinks I'm crazy, but I no longer discuss anything with him because he has become a stranger. "Man," he says at least once a day, "you're out of your mind. They *all* put out."

A few weeks, and a letter comes in the mail from my father. For some crazy reason my heart starts pounding, and I race up to Marty's and tear it open. Stand by the window and read . . . but there is nothing to read. Just five neatly typed pages of figures. Dollars and cents. Expenditures . . . on me. He has gone through all his cancelled checks and given them to his secretary to type out. Item: ten thousand dollars for David's education. Item: two thousand dollars for the dentist. Item: specialists for the back injury, and clothing bills, and three thousand dollars for summer camp, and—oh, you bastard—my allowance listed for the past ten years. What are you trying to tell me, Leo? That I am an ungrateful boy? No, what you are saying, though you don't know it, is that your investment has not paid off. You bought an expensive stock that went bust, and now you are mad as hell about it. But not as mad as I am. Nor as hurt. As I burn those pages and sit down to write you the cruellest letter of my life. *Wrong.* Tear it up. That is just what he wants: a reaction so he can continue the war. Sorry, Dad, the enemy has taken the war away.

(Somewhere a guitar is playing, not amplified, just a

plain old guitar down the hall. And outside my window laundry flutters over the back fence. Miles and miles of laundry making me feel that I am on a ship, white sails. There is even a seagull riding the wind to 4th Street. Yes, Mr. Tambourine Man, you can play a song for me, because Maggie is eating breakfast with Pablo, our dog, and there are flowers in the green jar, and all that I am writing about is behind me. Not solved, but over at least, with a summer day to live and the laundry a good omen and Pablo eating a fried egg. The story I write is not the whole story, the past only, while the future comes today in a sea of white laundry and a lazy guitar down the hall. I have lived so many lives, but for this moment I know a sudden happiness. Maggie in a yellow dressing gown with hair about her shoulders. A sooty bird on the windowsill. A world . . . of sunlight.)

He came back after one letter and three postcards. And when I opened the door I hardly knew him, because he was tan and very blond and his hair was shorter. White slacks and a blue shirt. We stood there for a moment, all kinds of feelings getting in the way: shyness, anticipation, a strange formality. He glanced around Marty's pad, smiling at the art nouveau posters and bentwood chairs. Smiling . . . yet not smiling at all.

He was so different, like something out of *Esquire,* and he wasn't meeting my eyes. Just glancing around the room and looking at the books and smiling a false smile. Finally I gave him a Coke and we sat down like two men at a club. I couldn't understand it—because I knew that he had waited for this moment too, and now he was avoiding me.

"You look great," I said after a few seconds. "Very healthy."

"Yeah, I know. Lots of sailing up there."

"You have a good time?"

"Pretty good."

"Any kids?"

"Sure. All social register and staunch Republicans."

I laughed. "Sounds marvelous. I'm . . . I'm glad you're back. It's been kind of rough here."

"Seen your father?"

"No. He doesn't phone anymore, either. It's strange —not living at home."

"Making the hippie scene?"

"God, no. It's a drag. Everyone's so damn immature."

"Some kid downstairs tried to sell me acid. Couldn't have been more than fifteen."

"I know. The place is crawling with them . . ." I could hear my own voice and it sounded so phony that I couldn't stand it. "Rick? Listen, I've really missed you. Did everything work out?"

"What?"

"The scene with your folks. Did they take the news all right?"

He gave a funny smile. "Well, not exactly."

"Tell me."

Then he looked at me—for the first time. "I don't know how to tell you. That's the problem."

"You can tell me anything, you know that. What happened? Did they raise hell?"

"To put it mildly—yes."

"So?"

"They refused."

"Refused? Refused what?"

"To let me go on with the C.O. thing. The draft board turned my application down."

"I don't understand. You never . . ."

"I know. I never wrote you about it. It was too much of a mess. But they turned the application down weeks ago, and my father won't let me appeal."

"That's crazy. You can appeal for months—years, even."

"Sure I can, but if I lose the case I go to jail. And that's what my father is afraid of."

I jumped to my feet. "You mean he'd rather see you in Vietnam? That's *insane!"*

"Davy, look, you don't really know my father . . ."

"The whole thing is insane. I don't even understand it. OK, OK. Call Harvard and tell them you're coming."

"My mother tried that, but it's too late. Admissions are closed."

I was pacing the room now. "Well then, to hell with them both. Tell them you won't go. They can't *make* you go."

"Davy, please sit down. You're not going to understand any of this if you don't listen. Look—my mother had decided to have a family reunion this summer. All our relatives came up to Newport, and the minute they arrived the pressure started. Treating me like a prodigal son, complimenting me for getting into Harvard. Christ, I was swamped—parties, picnics, going out on the boat every day—and the longer it went on, the less I could tell them the truth. But when I heard from the draft board, I knew I had to. So one night at dinner, when everyone was in a good mood, I told them about my letter to Harvard and the C.O. application—and my father went white. He asked how I intended to get out of such a mess, and I said, well, I'll appeal. Then he asked what I'd do if I lost the case—and when I said that I'd go to jail before I'd go into the army, he hit the roof."

"So what? So the hell what?"

"Let me finish! From that day on, he wouldn't let up. The whole damn family agreed with him and the pressure was awful. My mother in tears, my grandfather yelling at me. . . . My father kept saying that he'd see me dead before he'd see me in jail, that a record would spoil my life, that no son of his was going to be a convict, that it would ruin his reputation in business . . ."

"He must be crazy!"

"No. The terrible thing is that he thinks he's right. You don't understand my father—he was an officer in Korea."

"But . . ."

"The letter to Harvard was a kind of betrayal. So now he's paying me back, making me do the honorable thing. For me to refuse induction . . ."

"You've always been a pacifist! He knew that!"

"This is different. Jail . . . is very different."

"You could *win* the appeal."

"He's convinced I won't. Don't you see? He's worried about his job, his friends, what people will say."

"All right—what about Canada?"

"I can't spend my whole life in Canada. You know that."

"So you're going into the army?"

"Yes. I guess I am."

I am sitting by the river with Ben. Thirteen years old and miserable and turning to Ben, counting on him, loving him, all my trust focused on his kind face and wise smile because Uncle Benjamin will never let me down or betray me.

"Davy?"

"Yes."

"I know how this is hurting you . . ."

"No, it's OK."

My father has been unfaithful to my mother, and Ben is the only one I can turn to. A man of perfect truth and honesty who will listen to what I have to say and advise me. Nothing can happen to me because of Benjamin.

"I'm letting you down. I know that."

"It's OK."

"It won't be so terrible. Maybe I can get reclassified and work with the medics. I won't kill people. I couldn't."

And then—as though the veering green Hudson River sky had opened to pour light upon him—I saw him as he was. Dishonest, a failure. Wind and sunlight. Wind whipping his muffler and sunlight casting silver on the waves. Dogs barking, a red kite, and oh God, please let me get away from here before I start crying again.

"You . . . you shouldn't have counted on me so much, Davy. There are certain things a person can't change, times when other people are stronger. But I won't kill anyone. I'll join a medical unit."

"I have to go now," I said abruptly. "I'm meeting Marty on 8th Street."

"Will you call me tomorrow? Maybe we can go to a gallery."

"Sure."

"Promise?"

"Sure. I'll call you."

He walked to the door and took a last look around the place, his isolation showing in his eyes, his loneliness at leaving me in the midst of a life that he would have no part of. For one terrible second I knew that I would never see him again. Death by fire—my childhood fear—trapped in fire, unable to get out. But it passed as I opened the door and said that I would call him.

I never called him. And whenever he phoned, I was busy. Dozens of excuses until he left for basic training, and wrote me letters that I never answered, and phoned me before he shipped out—only I wasn't home—and sent one last letter saying how nobody in his outfit believed in the war. None of them: the kids from the north and the kids from the south, black and white, farmers and intellectuals, mechanics and poets. Saying how not one of them believed in the war, and how they just got drunk all the time and talked about sex, trying to hold onto their courage because they were off to fight President Johnson's stinking little war that no one believed in.

And then he was dead.

I see him standing in the doorway . . . his isolation showing in his eyes, his loneliness at leaving me in the midst of a life that he would have no part of. I see him turn and walk down the stairs . . . I see him pause at the bottom and wave at me . . . I didn't wave back. Five minutes later I went to sit in the park, no appointment with Marty, just a desire to be alone. It was all so clear, so beautifully, ironically clear, what had happened to Richard Heaton the third. This rebel and pacifist and intellectual, who was responsible for my new-found adulthood, had become a child again. A little boy who would obey his father when the chips were down, tremble and obey him even if the price was death, because childhood ties were stronger than ideals. All those years of terror and admiration, parental dictatorship and authority, had brainwashed him into believing that the old man was right. One couldn't let the old man down, the parent-king, the mythical god. He could have done so many things. Appealed the decision. Gone to jail. Found a new life in Canada. There were a hundred ways out. (God! I judge him even now, take upon myself a righteousness, blame him . . . when all the blame is mine.) So soft in the park, a gentle twilight with street lights blinking on and people coming home from work. A few hippies, a cop walking his beat. And I sit there realizing that I am alone now, alone for the first time in my life. I hear him talking to me about Leo—don't hate him, Davy, just act like an adult, break the ties—and it is all so funny and sad, the way things work out. Perhaps we have switched identities and it is he who sits on this bench, free at last, while I am off to Vietnam. Because that is the way it should have been. . . .

A man sits down beside me. I glance at him and see a square worried face with glasses. Neat business suit. Striped tie.

"Sonny?"

"Yeah. What?"

"I wonder if you could help me?"

He takes a photograph out of his square blue suit and shows it to me, mumbling in his square Midwestern accent. In the photograph is a nice little teen-age girl in a white dress. Blonde.

"Do you know this girl? Ever seen her down here?"

"No," I say.

"Are you sure? Her name is Gloria Williams."

Another parent looking for his kid in the Village. Looking for his little girl who was so pretty in her graduation dress, but who would be unrecognizable to him now —if he could find her. I shake my head.

"Are you sure? Her friends think she's come down here. Been missing for two weeks. She's . . . she's only seventeen."

"Sorry," I say. So blond and pretty, posing in her white dress and smiling at the photographer in . . . where? Ohio? Michigan? Why did you run away, Gloria? He doesn't know, but I do. And I suddenly realize that wherever you are, you are better off than with this so-well-intentioned man who has tried to erase your soul.

He offers me a dollar. "Thanks anyway, son."

I refuse the money and walk away, leaving him with his photograph and his sadness and his guilt and all the things he should have done differently. When I get home Marty is in the kitchen reading a copy of the *East Village Other*. He stares at the look on my face.

"Marty," I say slowly. "Will you take me to Cowboy's?"

THE CLOCK WILL HELP me. If I can just keep staring at it, I will not lose my sense of time. I will not drown in time like the last trip, but hold it steady. Please, God, give me the truth of who I am—but do not let me drown.

"Ready, Little David?" asks Cowboy. Yes, I say, but I want to hold this alarm clock. "You scared?" Yes, I say. Cowboy puts his arm around me. "Son, a trip is only what you want it to be. You expected bad things the last time, so you freaked. This time will be better." I stare at him. Will you bring me down if I ask? "Oh yes, Little

David. Surely."

I look at the others—Marty, Chester and Happy-time—and they smile. Cowboy's pad is lit with candles and we are sitting on mattresses. Walls hung with paisley, soft music on the stereo. My second trip. I swallow the acid cap, 250 mikes, and lean against the wall holding my clock. It is very quiet. Happytime puts her kitten on my lap. 10:00 p.m. I stroke the kitten and wait . . . wait . . . as the music plays and people smile. Someone puts a joint in my mouth. I drag on it, trying to relax. The kitten is asleep and I am unwinding, drowsy almost. 10:42. Oh . . . yes. It has started. The candlelight turns to gold and spills across the table. Soft gold dripping onto the floor. Inching its way across the floor onto my foot. Warm, liquid gold. So pretty. And . . . oh, the room is coming to life now. The room is breathing. Flowers are growing through the walls. Everything is beginning to breathe and flower and come to life and . . . oh, God . . . the light, the light is spilling through the air like colored glass. Every color, every piece of light . . . is showering down on me. A glass waterfall. I snap my fingers and blue sparks come from them. I hold my hands before me and a separate color grows from each finger. I am flowering like the room and growing colors . . . I breathe and the colors of my breath spill down my shirt, magenta, blue, and gold. The floor is swimming and pulsating with orange liquid. The room breathes in and out, and an emerald rain showers me . . . perfection . . . music washing over me in silver waves, carrying me on billows of silver. 11:25. The kitten on my lap has crawled into my belly. A thing of love, my belly opening and the kitten crawling inside. I feel it breathe with my breathing and the rivers of our blood flow together. Bells . . . each reverberation lifts me. The bells chime and I ride their cadences. The bells are rocking me. I sit inside the bells and rock with them, back and forth. The kitten flows out of my body, a soft wet thing, and I hold it before me seeing every separate atom and molecule . . . seeing that it is not a kitten but a pulsing heart in the heart of the universe. My clock . . . its numbers are blood and the hands have stopped.

All the colors have flowed back into the candle. The flame envelopes and holds them. The world has ended. Marty's face has vanished, sucked back into Universal Time. Cowboy has no eyes. And now . . . now I can hear the universe breathing, and the sounds of all the birds in the world as they fly, and the wash of every ocean on every beach. I can hear worms inching through the ground and the wings of butterflies. Everywhere, a whirring and whispering of creatures. Ocean, star and sand. Sunlight and eagle . . . The room has lifted and opened into Universal Time and I am not afraid. The colors have gone, and Time is dismembering me with love. One face . . . and it is my face. One cosmos . . . and it is me. I and flowing and pulsating with God. Time dismembers me and puts me back together. I am not my mind. I am nothing. I am . . . everything.

At dawn I stand by the window and watch the sunrise.

"So beautiful," I say to Cowboy. "So beautiful."

"The colors. Right, Little David?"

"And the bells," says Chester.

Happytime kisses me. "Oh Davy, we're so glad. You belong to us now."

I sleep for six hours and wake to find Chester snoring beside me, naked. Marty has gone to school, and Cowboy is sitting on the floor capping acid. He is dressed in faded levis, boots, and a ten-gallon hat. Happy is cooking breakfast in the kitchen.

HAPPY: Preacher says the macrobiotic diet makes you holy, and he's right. I've been holy for a week now. Preacher says the body and the soul are one.

COWBOY: Preacher's full of crap.

HAPPY: He isn't, Cowboy. Why are you so mean? Preacher's changed my whole life.

COWBOY: Why? Because he balled you?

HAPPY: Everything Preacher says is true.

CHESTER: (*mumbling*) Is the food ready?

COWBOY: Marty made two hundred bucks last week. Man, such a righteous cat. Two hundred bucks.

HAPPY: I don't care about money. Preacher says it's an illusion.

COWBOY: You know what I'm gonna do one of these days? I'm gonna get Preacher alone and shoot him so full of speed he don't come down for a month. And then I'm gonna castrate him.

HAPPY: I hate you, Cowboy.

COWBOY: Feeling's mutual. Are you awake, Davy? Chow's on.

(HAPPY *brings out a macrobiotic breakfast of rice and vegetables, and we eat it on the floor.* VALIANT *and* PREACHER, *who live downstairs, come in and join us.*)

VALIANT: Guess what?

CHESTER: What?

VALIANT: Tiny Alice gets in today.

COWBOY: No kidding. With Dormouse?

VALIANT: Yep. They got a ride all the way from the Haight.

HAPPY: You'll love her, Davy. Tiny is so groovy . . . and Dormouse is beautiful.

COWBOY: Yeah, but if he gets in my way he goes down with you, Valiant. I mean it. I got business to conduct.

VALIANT: Everything is business with you, man. Why don't you live for a change?

COWBOY: Listen, King Arthur—don't push your luck. If Marty and me didn't work, the rest of you would starve.

HAPPY: (*in an awed voice*) It's true, Cowboy. We forget it sometimes, but it's true.

CHESTER: Little David had a groovy trip last night. Didn't you, Little?

I nod and we eat. And none of them seem strange. Not Happy with her bad skin and dirty hair. Not Chester who looks like a water rat. Not Valiant who dresses like a medieval page. Not even Preacher in his clerical collar and long black coat. Today, for the first time, they do not . . . seem strange.

After breakfast Chester goes back to bed and I help Cowboy cap the acid. It is in plastic bags, mixed into a calcium compound, and we spoon it into gelatin capsules. A full bowl of capsules goes into the icebox for firming. Happy is baking bread, and Valiant and Preacher have gone down to catch the morning vibrations.

"You like Happy?" Cowboy asks me. Sure, I say. Why? "Stay away from her. She has clap." I start to laugh, and Cowboy smiles at me. "Well, someone's gotta protect you, Little David. Who'll protect you if Cowboy don't?"

Suddenly there is loud knocking at the door. Cowboy goes pale and rushes the acid into the kitchen, but it is only Valiant and Preacher who enter with their arms around a large blond girl. She is wearing several skirts like a gypsy and many strands of beads. Her feet are bare, and trailing behind her is a little kid three or four years old in a diaper.

COWBOY: Tiny! Hey, you look great, girl. Why did it take you so long?

TINY: You wouldn't believe what I've been through. You wouldn't *believe* it.

(TINY *drags in her shopping bags, and her child, and kisses* COWBOY *on the mouth.* HAPPY *comes out of the kitchen and soon everyone is kissing and hugging. Then* COWBOY *opens some beer to celebrate and we sprawl on mattresses.*)

TINY: You know how long it took me to cross the country? Three *weeks*. Mandrake's car kept breaking down. And Dormouse here with a cold, and me just shaking with terror. God, those Middle West vibrations! Creepy. Mandrake was stoned the whole trip.

CHESTER: How come you're back? When you split, you said good-bye forever.

TINY: Well, I was wrong, out of my mind. God, those

(*122*)

creeps in the Haight. Too much. Acid at inflated prices and everyone hustling on the street. Angels cutting up the spades—sheer paranoia. I had to come back for Dormouse's sake. It was really unhealthy. . . . Hey, who's this?

COWBOY: This here is Little David. A very sweet little cat.

TINY: (*looking me over*) He's cute. Collegiate, sort of. Well, I tell you, I am *glad* to be back. The atmosphere was terrible for Dormouse. A spade threatened to kidnap him because he said I burned him with bad acid—which wasn't true. Here, Dormouse honey, play with your coloring book. He likes to color. . . . Where was I? Oh, the Haight. Believe me, it isn't what they say it is. Come to San Francisco? Lies, lies. An atmosphere of total paranoia. Everyone worshiping those creepy Angels like they were God, and sociologists roaming the park making notes. Have you ever had venereal disease? one of them asked me. Sure, I said, haven't you? I swear, the whole thing's a fraud. . . .

I am no longer listening to her, but watching Dormouse. He is sitting on the floor in his diaper, coloring in a Mary Poppins coloring book. But the way he is coloring is strange. Circles and circles, over and over like a little machine. The look in his eyes is peculiar. I ask Tiny what is wrong with him.

TINY: Wrong with him? Nothing's wrong with him. He's on speed. Not a full dose, mind you, just a little tiny child-dose. It's good for him.

(*123*)

CHESTER: Are you sure? Meth could hurt him.

TINY: Not in little doses. And it makes him happy—doesn't it, Dormouse? God, I wish I were rich. I'd keep Dormouse high forever so he would never see the ugliness in the world. . . . Oh, listen, I forgot. The most *fantastic* thing happened before I left. I saw Carlton.

HAPPY: No!

TINY: It's true. Dormouse and I were walking down Stanyon Street and all of a sudden *Carlton* is walking towards us with this ugly chick. I mean, ugly. Do you know something? He didn't even recognize me. I had to introduce myself to him. And there is Dormouse, staring and staring, and Carlton doesn't know who he is. Doesn't even recognize his own kid! Thank God I never married him.

COWBOY: Listen, honey. Are you through with Mandrake?

TINY: Ugh, that creep.

COWBOY: OK. So why don't you be my old lady for a while? Melanie split for Chicago last month.

TINY: Really? Well . . . all right. I don't mind. Just as long as we don't get busted here. I don't want Dormouse to have a record.

(Easy. Like slipping into a bathtub when your muscles ache. Yet a part of me was standing above myself, looking down, watching myself slip into this warm warm tub. After the second trip none of them seemed strange, just like . . . a family. But God, so new to me: this world that had no tomorrows, where Dormouse stumbled around high while people smiled, and Cowboy played papa, and Tiny went naked, and Preacher gave sermons on the oneness of existence. Where everyone had instant happiness—pot, acid, speed—and talked about being "programmed" and threw the *I Ching* coins and studied astrology. No tomorrows. Just sex and dope and the Beatles playing and the factory grinding away, me a part of it now: learning to fix pot by removing the stems and seeds and shaking it through a strainer, then rolling it into colored papers. Marty, grinning at my conversion, egging me on. Why was I there? Loneliness, I guess, the terror of being alone in the world. . . . They *were* like a family. Cowboy, so protective—and Happy, so childish. Tiny Alice like an earth mother, offering to ball me one night. Won't Cowboy mind? I asked. "Oh, no," she said. "We all share one another. It's part of our thing." We smoked some pot and lay down on the mattress, but it wouldn't work. She wasn't mean about it, though. Just laughed and said that maybe girls weren't my trip. . . .)

I look at you, Maggie, and see the sunlight. I touch you, and know the world. The colors and the bells are you now—and when I finish this story I will show it to you. Not for approval, the way I used to show things, but from love. You have seen my dark places and still love me, and though I tried to run from you I always came back. Running . . . from Leo, from Mom, from Rick's long shadow as he went to war. Running—that's it. I was running and the acid stopped the race. Caught me in its arms and held me, suspended, transfixed. By October I had settled into the family, sleeping and painting at Marty's and spending the rest of my time at Cowboy's. Doing my share of the work in return for free acid. . . . What am

I trying to remember? Oh yes, Leo's new approach. I hadn't heard from him in weeks, when one day an envelope arrived in the mail. My first instinct was to tear it up, but then curiosity got the better of me. Wild, man. Absolutely wild. In the envelope was a check for ten dollars and a cheery little note. "Dear Davy, Why haven't your mother and I heard from you? You're busy, I suppose, but it wouldn't hurt to phone. Would you like to go to the theater next week? I have tickets for a musical which they say is pretty good. I have been wondering, also, about your clothes. Winter is coming and I'd like to buy you a new coat. I know you're not dressing like the other kids down there, hippie-style, because you're too smart for that. So how about the theater next Saturday and a shopping spree with the old man? (signed) Your devoted father." I started to laugh, and when I finished laughing I mailed the check back to him. . . . A few days later he sends me a newspaper clipping about some college out west where they have "free form" education and everyone does what he wants. "A new experiment in learning, with strong emphasis on the arts." A week after that he sends another check. Where did he think I was? Boarding school? Summer camp? From that day on, he never let up. Notes, postcards and checks. Newspaper clippings and travel brochures and a gift certificate from Saks Fifth Avenue (where the better hippies go).

Incredible—and yet so typical. If he'd had any guts he would have come down to the Village and faced me. But no, he didn't have the courage for that, so he did it through the mail. Ten bucks, then twenty. An offer of a coat, then a whole wardrobe. He even sent me a subscription to a new art magazine. Lesson number one in American Sociology: When you want your kid to do something, bribe him. But the bird had flown the nest, and now that it had wings there was no reason to come back. Like, you know, man, give me just one reason. . . . Even Ben, who used to be on my side, dropped in one day to persuade me to come home. OK, so I was a little high that afternoon, but what did he expect? He hadn't phoned me first. Just arrived at the door with a book of poetry, such a slender excuse . . . and I swear that he looked like something from another planet. A 1940's suit patched at the elbows, and an old leather briefcase, and the rimless spectacles. A character from Arthur Miller.

Well, Davy. It's been a long time, hasn't it?

Oh, indeed. Centuries. Have a seat, Ben. Have two seats.

What?

Make yourself at home, is what I mean. Groove on the atmosphere. How do you like my paintings?

Well . . . they're very different. Rather startling. How are you, my dear?

Deer: a four-footed animal known for its shyness.

I beg your pardon?

Nature. Don't you like nature? It's so innocent.

I don't under . . .

I know you don't, Ben. That's why I'm explaining it to you. You see, nature is one thing but man is another.

Davy, are you *on* something? Some kind of drug?

Let's flip for it. Heads I am. Tails I'm not.

Dear God . . .

Are you taking the name of the Lord in vain, Ben? Gee, I never thought you were like that. I always thought you were pious. No booze, no girls. Benjamin, I have spent my whole life wondering if you ever slept with a girl.

From bad to worse, until he left with tears in his eyes. And though he said he wouldn't tell Dad, he did—much later. Just couldn't keep the news to himself that I was having a few kicks. Just couldn't stand to see me happy. Well, if not happy then at least free from pain. I was beginning to understand why straight people loathed the hippies. Why they would do anything short of atomic war to put them down. Because hippies refused to play the game: the money game, the power game, the monogamy game. And like, if all those kids won't play, what happens to that great big profit machine that makes war and ulcers? But the real secret was envy. (How come those kids can ball everyone when I can't? How come they don't work when I have to commute every day? How come they enjoy themselves while *I* keep my nose to the grindstone?) Poor Mister Jones. One day you will wake up, at age fifty perhaps, and discover that you haven't lived at all. You will discover that you hate your wife and your kids and your job, and your power lawn mower, and your second mortgage, and a scream will stifle itself in your throat. . . .

OK, so I was changing—but only because I was

looking at people. Cowboy and Chester and Happy gave to one another without selfishness. Never cheated, never copped out, never betrayed a friend. Never hurt anyone under the guise of self-righteousness. Never interfered with another person's trip. Hell, it may be that I was always split about them, liking them one moment, alienated the next. But this fear of being alone. . . . They were always there for me: Happy cooking some crazy Zen meal, Tiny weaving rugs, Chester reading comic books, and Valiant and Preacher running in and out like town criers. The cops were around, the cops weren't around, stash the dope, no, bring it out. The only person who worried me was Dormouse, but eventually Cowboy took him over. Refused to let him eat the macrobiotic food and bought him milk and eggs. Cowboy had a wife and child in Arizona, and maybe Dormouse reminded him of his own kid. I don't know. . . . Pretty soon I adopted Dormouse too, and I would take him to the park a few times a week to get the sunshine. Such a sad little boy, he hardly ever spoke, and once when I tried to get him to play with some other kids, he just stared at me, bewildered. . . . Time —my sense of time had changed. Whole weeks would pass and I wouldn't know what day it was, or whether I'd slept or not. Long evenings of music—blankets and records and clothes all over the floor—and the sweet smell of pot drifting under the blue lights. Cowboy's family said they weren't hung-up on the past, but they always talked about it. . . .

TINY: You know why I left home? Because my mother said my skirts were too short. The town tease, hassling me about *skirts*. I hate that witch.

PREACHER: Hate is destructive, Tiny. Parents go through some ugly karma.

TINY: I don't care. She's still a witch.

COWBOY: Girl, you make me laugh. Sitting up there in Greenwich, Connecticut, complaining. I was raised in an orphanage, and if we had one square meal it was a trip. I liked them nuns, though. Very groovy chicks. You know what I'd do? I would sniff glue and get high on it, and then I'd walk around flashing on the sisters and their habits and their beads. Flashing and flashing, and hungry as an alley cat.

CHESTER: My father was an army officer.

VALIANT: (*sighing*) Yeah, we know.

CHESTER: Army camps, moving around, loading up the station wagon with junk. Man, did my mother love Sears Roebuck junk. I went to eight different schools until we settled in California, in one of those split-level jobs. Squaresville. Two cars in the driveway and everything.

COWBOY: But you ate. Right?

CHESTER: And then I had this revelation. When I was fourteen or something. Like, I suddenly saw that I was trapped in a big machine that made bombs and synthetic food and pink toilet paper. You know? Just a great big enriched-white-bread machine called America. So I split.

PREACHER: The vibrations are negative tonight.

TINY: She wouldn't even let me date.

VALIANT: Who?

TINY: My *mother*. The suburban prostitute. Boarding schools, summer camp, chaperones. If I even talked about boys, she would go pale. Like virginity was the Hope Diamond or something. God, I hate that phony.

HAPPY: (*dreamily*) My uncle died of cancer last week.

COWBOY: Oh, those straight cats and their cancer. They're really hung-up on it. You know? It's their ethnic disease. You ever see a hippie with cancer?

VALIANT: I did once. Skin cancer.

COWBOY: Naw, man—that was probably clap or something. Hippies don't get cancer because they aren't programmed for hate. Squares are programmed that way, so they get sick.

CHESTER: (*excited*) Yeah, it's true! Like, you take my old man and his ulcers. He wanted an army career for me, and when I said I wasn't interested he hit me. I cried. I really did.

HAPPY: My uncle tried to ball me once.

VALIANT: No, he didn't, Happy. You always say that.

HAPPY: Why are you so mean? He did try to ball me, but then my brother came home and everything, so he couldn't. At least, I *think* he tried to ball me. But he never let us go to the movies, and I wanted to be a movie star.

COWBOY: Ha ha.

HAPPY: Well, I could have been a movie star if anyone had let me.

PREACHER: In the oneness of time, such things don't matter.

COWBOY: You give me a pain, Preacher.

PREACHER: (*smiling*) That's because I'm getting to you.

COWBOY: You'll flip first. . . . Say, you know what? I

heard from Jeannie yesterday. How that broad located me, I will never know, but she writes and says that she needs bread, and the kid is sick, and the basement is flooded. Well, I had to laugh about that.

TINY: *(absorbed)* So I started dating spades to get even with her, and then she said she'd disinherit me. Disinherit! I was really insulted. Like, who would *want* her lousy money in the first place. Then she said I couldn't wear her fur coat anymore. Big deal. You know what I did? I took that crummy mink and threw it out the window. And it landed on the postman. Wild, wild. The postman standing there in a state of shock, mink all over his head. . . . You're so quiet, Davy. Why did *you* leave home?

Everyone is looking at me, their eyes drifting through a blue haze. Looking at me with great interest. I try to concentrate on her question—why did *you* leave home—but oddly enough, I cannot remember. Weird, so very weird. I cannot . . . remember why.

Time. Days that are minutes and weeks that are years. Time, expanding and contracting. I had loved the seasons once, and now I didn't notice them. Didn't notice the weather getting colder, or the first snowflakes, or the Christmas decorations on 8th Street. I was painting five hours a day and the rest of the time was a blank. Go to Cowboy's, come back from Cowboy's. Take money from the savings account and buy Dormouse a snowsuit. . . . A week before Christmas Mom called and asked me to come home for the holidays, but I said no and hung up. So of course she had to send a package. Package? It was a *carton,* bursting with presents, all shapes and sizes, and everything wrapped in gold paper. To Davy with love from Dad. To Davy with love from Mother. To Davy . . . I didn't open them. Just took them out to the street and gave them away to passing kids. The Hippie Santa. On Christmas Eve we made a human Christmas tree out of Chester. First we decorated him with little lights and popcorn and paper ornaments—and then we plugged him in and sang *Joy To The World.* He really looked great standing there with his arms raised. It was the first time I'd ever seen Dormouse smile. . . . But Christmas day was a blank because we were all stoned, Chester asleep with his lights twinkling. . . .

Then it was New Year's Eve.

Mom phoned at nine p.m. Exactly at nine. It was snowing. And her voice sounded strange. I didn't know what she was talking about, didn't even hear her. She kept repeating it, her voice trembling. Repeating the words which I couldn't understand because I didn't want to understand them. Then I heard the words . . . and got the meaning . . . and stood there listening to her . . . as I realized that Rick was dead. Killed in action. The helicopter shot down. Mrs. Heaton had phoned, hysterical. Killed in action. The helicopter destroyed . . . I didn't say anything for a long time because there was nothing to say. No feelings, no thoughts . . . but finally I had to say something, so I asked her if Rick had killed anyone before he died. "What, Davy?" Did he kill anyone? I asked. Did he murder anyone? "I don't understand." Never mind, I said, it's OK. Really. I'm not upset. "Davy—do you want me to come down there and be with

you? I could take a cab." No, Mother, it's OK. Good-bye.
. . . Hang up the phone. Sit down. Light a cigarette and
watch the snow. That's all, just watch the snow. . . . I
couldn't feel anything, so I put on my jacket and went
outdoors. People were drunk, getting ready for midnight,
whole swarms of them reeling down the sidewalk. And
suddenly I wanted to be drunk too, drunk on alcohol like
the squares, but I didn't have any money. So I walked up
to a man and asked him for some. It seemed quite natural, hitting this square old man for a few bucks. Nothing
wrong with it. He smiled and gave me what he thought
was a dollar, but it turned out to be ten and I didn't tell
him. Didn't even thank him, just took the money and hur-
ried away. Into a liquor store and buy some scotch. Sit on
the curb and drink it. Nothing. No feelings. Drink some
more, Davy, after all it's New Year's. . . . Finally I got
a little high and it felt good, so I decided to phone Rick's
father. The more I thought about it, the better the idea
seemed. Into a phone booth and dial the number. Because after all it is New—Year's—Eve.

Hello?

Mr. Heaton?

Yes.

This is Davy, Mr. Heaton. David Marks. How are
you?

(silence)

Are you there, Mr. Heaton?

Yes, David. I'm here.

(*134*)

Listen, Mr. Heaton, I just called up to wish you Happy New Year. And to say how sorry I am about your son and everything. A real inconvenience.

What? What did you say?

Yep, it must be a real inconvenience. Funerals are so depressing.

Davy? What's the matter with you? Have you . . .

But if you want to invite me to the funeral, I don't think I can make it. My clothes are too shabby.

Now look here! If you don't think I'm . . .

Oh, I know you're upset, Mr. Heaton. I know that. But what I suggest is this: Just take the wife on a Caribbean cruise and the two of you will get over it. Right? Buy her a diamond watch or something. Get a new car.

God damn you! What are you saying to me?

Buy a yacht or an airplane or something. And you'll get over it right away. It's so funny, Mr. Heaton, so funny. You killed your own son and you probably don't even know it. Don't even know that you killed your own. . . .

(he had hung up)

Snow . . . falling on me like feathers. Light, bright feathers. And I am warm now, the booze warming me nicely. Where shall I go to celebrate New Year's? I don't know, so I shall just keep walking with my friendly bottle of scotch. Fourth Street, Third Street, Second Street. Downtown. Yes, downtown. Where Mr. Heaton works. Oh . . . yes. A groovy idea. Celebrate New Year's on Wall Street. What a splendid idea. Because where, oh where in the world is the spirit of America better exemplified than on Wall Street? Groovy. A New Year's Eve on the street of walls. . . . Walking, stumbling, but not cold, even though my shoes are soaked and my hair is heavy with snow. Everyone is celebrating but Chinatown. They have a different New Year, I guess. Do they celebrate New Year's in Vietnam? Maybe they send champagne down with the napalm. Now there is an interesting idea: attach a little hat and noise-maker to every bomb. Happy New Year from Uncle Sam! Silent Snow, Secret Snow—a story I read once. Silent snow . . . falling on the young soldiers. But maybe it doesn't snow in Vietnam. I don't know anything about that country at all. Should have read up on it, should have prepared myself for this crisis in World Events. I don't even read the *New York Times:* all the news that's print to fit. . . . Oh, how nice. I am on Wall Street. And it is empty. Quite beautifully empty, not even a footprint in the snow. High high buildings. Narrow narrow streets. "Hello!" I call. No answer. Where has America gone? Home to get drunk, dragging its money behind it. I shall sit down in the middle of Wall Street. No, *lie* down in the middle of Wall Street, prostrating myself to America. . . . Columbia, gem of the ocean, I am prostrating myself because you are stronger than I am. You beautiful money factory, you assembly line of can openers, you universal dime store. You have guts, while basically I am chicken. . . . Chicken Little said the sky was falling and everyone believed her. What a camp. This silly chicken starts a rumor and everyone freaks out. I am beginning to dig nursery rhymes because psychological truths are concealed in them. Take Simple Simon. Was he really that dumb? No, he was merely blocked—an underachiever with regressive tendencies. Miss Muffet too. And Mary Mary. And Tom, the piper's son, who could only play one little song. . . .

He's dead.

The boy I loved is dead.

I got back to Cowboy's at dawn, shaking, my cheeks on fire. And I was sick, only I didn't know it. I thought they'd all be there—Marty, Cowboy, everyone—but the pad was empty. Pale sunshine coming through the window, some beer cans on the floor. Then I saw Dormouse. He was sitting in the corner of the room holding an eggbeater. "Hi, Dormouse," I said. "Happy New Year." He didn't say anything, just kept turning the handle, watching the beaters rotate. "That's a nice eggbeater. Can I play with it too?" He shook his head, and all of a sudden he seemed like a very old man. Some old senile man sitting in a rest home, turning the handle of an eggbeater. "It's 1968, Dormouse. A new year. Don't you want to play with me?" Nothing. Not a look or a nod, just nothing. A little old dead man. Suddenly I knew that I would kill myself if Dormouse didn't talk to me, go into the kitchen and cut my wrists—so I found a joint in the ashtray, and lit it, and sat down on the floor facing him. He sniffed at the sweet smell. Then he looked at me as I drew the smoke into my lungs and held it there. Progress. "You want a puff?" I asked, and he nodded. I gave him one, and I had one, and soon we were sharing the joint. A kind of communication. . . . The grass hit me hard, very quick, spacing the room out and making a ribbon of time. I lay down and put my head in his lap. He stiffened a little but didn't move, and as I sank into wherever I was going, I smiled at him. "You high yet? You high yet . . . Dormouse?"

(After a while there were no reasons. I was high or I wasn't high. I worked or I didn't. In bed with the flu I'd gotten New Year's, then out of bed. But no different. In or out, awake or asleep, nothing mattered. It was worse than grief, this knowledge that I had abandoned him. He had died alone—and it didn't matter that everyone dies alone, because he wasn't everyone, just a single boy. I had wanted to hurt him and had succeeded, loving and hating him all at once, judging him for leaving me, condemning him for being weak . . . as I am weak. I can't remember February. Or March. Did I . . . no, I didn't work after March because I was bum-tripping. Bum-tripping yet unable to stop. Freaking-out yet taking more acid. And I can ask why and why and why . . . and the answer is always the same. Don't know. Cowboy started talking me down, and when that didn't work he used Thorazine. He even suggested that I stop for a while, but I couldn't stop because . . . hell, I simply do not know. Maybe because a bad trip was better than no trip. Even the times when I thought my eyes were popping out and floating through the door. Even the times I would crouch in the bathtub watching my smile trickle down the drain. And the time when I felt my legs turn to marble and begged for someone to chip me loose. And the time when I saw myself dwindle to a dot on the floor, smaller and smaller, to the size of an ant. And the very special time when I took acid and speed together and felt the world rush in on me like a locomotive, screaming and hurtling past my ears, dragging me into a nightmare of sound-touch-taste-sight, the levels of reality too numerous and terrible to endure . . . even then, I did not want to stop. In April I did a strange thing: took the bus up Riverside Drive and rode past the apartment house. Rode past it, got off at the corner and walked back, looking at Leo's and Mom's apartment. So funny, because the doorman didn't recognize me. Bob Ryan, who used to fix my bike and take me to the zoo. . . . I stood there for a long time, smelling the spring and the river and watching the sun glint on the windows of the building. A clear red sunset, the sound of tugboats . . . and I kept trying to feel what I felt. Remorse? Regret? Loneliness? No, none of those things. I just felt like a person who knows he is going to die, so he goes back to his old home for a last look. You go back hoping that the bittersweet sense of your childhood will return, but it doesn't—because the childhood was inside you, not in the place, and you cannot recapture it. I stared at Bob Ryan, but he gave me an irritable look—ugh, hippies—and turned away. So I went back to the Village and forgot about it . . . and got high again.)

Where were you, Leo? All the time your little boy was going insane? Well, you were sitting in your office writing me notes about the weather and the stock market, and what the Lowensteins were doing, and what movie you'd seen recently, and say, Davy, why don't we get together next week and go to a ball game? Just like the old

days, huh? . . . No, man. Too easy. Too much of a cop-
out. If you'd cared what was happening to me, you would
have come down. You were still sending checks and
travel brochures, still finding new and interesting col-
leges, but not once did you come down. Mom did, and I
almost freaked trying to act straight for her, being a bit
high at the time, but served her coffee and cake nonethe-
less. And Ben came several times to talk about "maturity" and "responsibility" and "the feelings of others."
But you, Leo, you just didn't come. . . . What is it like
to go insane? Shall I tell you the truth? To go insane is
like falling into a swimming pool full of hornets. You are
on the diving board (thinking, of course, that there is
water down there) so you smile at the world, flex your
muscles and dive. BZZZZZZZ. Oh, Jesus. Oh, Lord.
What's *happened* to me? Something's stinging me! Oh
God, get me out of here. I'm drowning in hornets!
They're all *over* me. Up my nose, in my crotch, in my
mouth and eyes. Somebody help me! *Please.* I'm being
stung to death. . . . Other things too. Like urinating
and seeing black ink stream out of your body. Like taking a bite of sandwich and discovering that it's dung. Like
sneezing and watching violet-colored pus spray out of
your nose. To go crazy, Leo, is not to enter a snake pit,
but to enter yourself. I saw—oh, I saw now—what I
really was. A walking bottle of pus and blood. A clear
plastic bag of dung. A garbage pail of unspeakable rem-
nants that were called David. I got high to escape this
person, and crashed into him again. Came down to escape this person, and saw him in the mirror. Like, you
know, I don't want to be dramatic or anything, but I was

going through an experience called The Return Trip. A charming phenomenon in which you start flashing on things days after you've been high. *Days.* In other words, Daddy dear, my brains were getting scrambled.

And then . . . the party.

Yes.

Cowboy had talked about it for weeks—the Mother's Day party he was going to give. A swinging event for everyone he knew: hippies and squares, Puerto Ricans and blacks, students and bums. A real bash. And all in honor of Mother's Day, because everyone has had a mother and should respect them. Tiny and Happy were going to be Mothers Of Honor because they had children —and the fact that Happy's kid was nowhere in evidence, because it had been taken away from her long ago, didn't seem to matter. . . . We were all very excited about the party and everyone contributed something. Cowboy contributed the dope, and Preacher wrote a sermon on Motherhood, and Valiant and Chester went out and shoplifted a lot of imitation flowers. Plastic or something, with glossy green leaves. So the pad became a kind of plastic bower and looked very freaky and nice.

It started early . . . swarms of people flocking in the door . . . and many of them were dressed as children. Hair ribbons and dolls. Lollipops. The only rule was No Noise, because Cowboy didn't want to attract the heat, so we all complied and behaved with a dignity befitting the occasion. Dozens of people sitting down on mattresses and lighting up, and grooving on the plastic flowers, and chatting with each other. Very very nice. Marty noticed that there were more cockroaches than usual in the kitchen and he suggested that we turn them on—because after all, cockroaches are mothers too—but no one could catch any, so we just let them scurry around. The Beatles were playing (in honor of the roaches) and Happy had made a Mother's Day cake with hashish in it. Everyone blew out a candle in honor of his mother, and the whole thing was quite dignified. Preacher was stoned on Nembutal, but determined to give his sermon anyway. He staggered forward and raised his hands.

My friends, I am here tonight to speak of. . . . My friends. I have come here tonight to address you on certain matters pertaining to . . . mothers. Yes. Because mothers and . . . *motherhood* are closely connected. If you will look at them closely, that is. To divide the . . . the mother from the child is virtually impossible because . . . well, consider the uterine experience in which a child's karma begins. An unravelling of threads, as it were, a unified thing which . . .

Everyone was listening attentively, Tiny with Dormouse on her lap, Happy sitting on the bureau—but suddenly Preacher passed out and sank to the floor. End of sermon. Valiant had brought tops to remind us of Innocent Childhood Days, and several people started spinning them. Cowboy was dressed as Whistler's Mother and began telling stories of what Whistler was like as a boy. ("A very disobedient cat. Would never brush his teeth.") Happy was serving Mother's Day cake, and Marty and some chick I didn't know were necking in the corner.

. . . Every so often Cowboy would remind people about the noise, but everyone was getting stoned and didn't care, and some black girl with wonderful African-looking hair turned the music up and a couple of kids started dancing. It was quite a nice party, with everyone doing his thing, and nobody hassling anybody, and Dormouse even smiled a few times. A very nice party, all in all. . . . But then Cowboy got hung up on the noise, so we silenced everyone and said that the Main Attraction was ready—which turned out to be Valiant and Happy, who stepped into the middle of the room and bowed. People sat down and waited to see what would happen. And what happened was that Happy took off her clothes and lay down on the floor and Valiant began to paint her. Not crudely —because Valiant had once been a fabric designer—but delicately, starting at her toes. He had many pots of paint and he wanted to turn Happy into a flower doll, daisies on her toes, vines up her legs, and roses on her belly. . . . The only trouble was that Happy was very high and couldn't stop giggling. I don't know what she was on, pot or Mother's Day cake, but it made her giggle and squirm and Valiant couldn't keep her still. Cowboy got a paint-brush and entered the act, and Chester and Marty did the same, and soon many people were bending over Happy-time, trying to keep her still so they could paint flowers on her. She kept saying that the brushes tickled, but nobody paid attention because everyone wanted to add a rose or a leaf and turn Happytime into a flower doll for Mother's Day.

I was sitting against the wall, and though I had been smoking, I wasn't high—just numb and distant. Once again I was watching myself, and I felt like two people. No, three. One of these people was a child, and one was an old man, and one was a corpse. Quite interesting, really. I saw the three of them with one eye, and with the other eye I watched Happytime. She was beginning to get tired, but Cowboy wouldn't let her go. Just held her down so everyone could paint her, and the harder he held her down, the more frightened she became. "Please!" she kept saying. "Please!" But nobody listened, because a dozen hands were painting her breasts and arms and mouth and cheeks and forehead and nobody wanted to stop. It was too much fun to stop. She was screaming now, so Cowboy stuffed a rag in her mouth and told her to shut up. Then she panicked and started kicking, but Cowboy just held her tighter as the hands kept painting and painting and Happytime's wild little eyes darted around the room. One of her ears was pink and the other was green. Roses on her nipples. . . . Suddenly I wanted to throw up. Wanted to be sick more than anything in the world. Wanted to run out of the room. Wanted to kill Cowboy—oh yes, please let me kill him—yet did nothing because I was trapped and paralyzed and could not move. . . .

A hand took mine and held it. Hard. I turned and saw a girl sitting next to me with a puppy on her lap. A girl with dark hair and green eyes. She was holding my hand so tightly that it hurt, but the touch . . . the touch was like life to me, so I gripped her hand back. Tears started coming down her face, and I gripped her even harder—life flowing through our fingers to one another, contact, hardness, warmth, meaning, flesh. Two hands.

. . . I don't know how long we sat there, Maggie, our hands locked like drowning people, but finally you turned to me and said, "Get me out of here. *Please.*" I helped you to your feet, and took the puppy from you, and led you out of the pad. You stopped in the hall and lit a cigarette, trembling. Where do you want to go? I asked. "My place. It's only two blocks." We went down the stairs, me holding the puppy in one arm, my other around your shoulder, and walked east, not speaking.

I didn't know who you were . . . all I knew was that the night and the sky and the city-smell of spring were the only things I wanted at that moment—because they were connected to you. Your shoulder was warm under my hand, and I could not take my hand away. We stopped for a red light and I asked, Is this your dog? "No, I found it on the street. But I want to keep it." Your voice was defiant, so I said, OK, we'll keep it . . . and the funny thing, Maggie, is that I said "we." In a few minutes we were going up a flight of stairs into a loft. Large and very clean, with posters on the wall and a dressmaker's dummy in the corner. An empty loft that didn't seem empty because there were flowers in jars and yellow cushions on the bed. The brick walls were whitewashed and the floor was dark blue, and I liked that. . . . You took the puppy from me and went to the refrigerator and got some milk. Poured it into a saucer and watched the dog lap it up. What kind of dog is it? I asked. "I don't know. It's alive." And I knew what you meant, because we had just emerged from a graveyard and a living thing seemed good. As the loft did, and the spring night. As you did—moving from the refrigerator to the stove. I watched you and saw a thin girl with long hair parted in the middle. White blouse and short denim skirt. Sandals, and legs that were tan . . . and then I looked away. You made instant coffee and brought two mugs over to the window, and we sat down. Neither of us drank the coffee, and for a long while there was nothing to say. Then you glanced at me.

"What will happen to her?"

"Who?"

"The girl they were painting. What will they do to her?"

"Have some kicks, I guess. That's all."

"Will they hurt her?"

"No. It was just a game, just kicks."

"Then why were you shaking?"

"I don't know. I felt sick suddenly."

"Me too. I wanted to die. They're zombies till they turn on, and then they're sadists. The love generation. . . . Why were you there?"

"I live with them."

"Really? I can't see you living with them."

"Why?"

"I don't know. You seem different. I was watching you when the party began, and you looked like someone in a foreign country who can't read the street signs. You kept squinting at things."

"I had a headache."

We fell silent, and you took out a cigarette but couldn't find a match, so I lit it for you. For some reason I could not look you in the eyes. You seemed too close.

"Do you like living with them?"

"Sure. Why not?"

"They're dead men, that's why. I came down here and all I found were dead people."

"You don't understand them."

"What is there to understand? They're dead, so they turn on to exist. I don't hate them—just what they do to each other. That little boy . . ."

"Dormouse? Don't worry about him. He's OK."

"He's *not* OK. He walks around like a puppet."

"Look—why are you so critical? You don't even know us."

"I live down here, remember? God, I'm not being holy or anything. I've done the same things they have. I couldn't stand myself the next morning, that's all."

"Then get your head straightened out!"

"What?"

"Straighten your head!"

"Why are you shouting at me?"

"I don't know! Just get your head fixed! Christ, I hate people who can't understand things. Why can't people like you understand things? Criticizing and criticizing —and no reasons. None of you have reasons for anything. Just one great big putdown. . . ."

You walked over to me. And then, Maggie, I felt your arms around me, holding me as I shook. Standing above me, cradling my head. "What's your name?" you asked softly. David, I said. . . . You stroked my hair, and kissed me, and I held onto you because you were the only thing left in the world and I could not let you go. Then I stood up and put my arms around you, and touched you, and kissed your mouth, and you asked me if

(*147*)

I wanted you and I said yes . . . but the moment we lay down together my fears returned, the fears I had had for a lifetime, and I wanted to run. I was cold as ice, knowing that it wouldn't work, knowing that I couldn't say the words but that you would find out anyway. And never in my life had I felt so alone. But you surprised me, because you stopped kissing and looked up at me, holding my face in your hands. No one had ever looked at me so simply, or deeply, and I was afraid. Because whatever you wanted, I could not give it—and I was alone. "Let's go to sleep," you said. Are you sure? I mumbled, wanting to believe you, wanting so badly. . . . "Yes, I'm sure. Put your arms around me." A sigh came out of me as though I had been in mortal danger, a sigh so deep and relieved that you smiled. And curled down in my arms, and lay your head on my shoulder. "Go to sleep, David." Not Davy, but David—a new sound in my ears—and now truly and deeply asleep, all at once like a child, dark hair spilling over your face and one hand holding mine. So I slept too, and slept well for the first time in months, the thin lithe form of you fitting my arms and the little bed large enough for us both. Slept. And dreamed of a field of white lilacs and a green sea flowing beyond. Black sand and a field of white lilacs, not growing on trees but scattered somehow, making paths to the sea. . . . And woke then at dawn, rested and peaceful, no surprise finding you in my arms. No surprise, just knowing that it was all right now, because I had slept, and you were still sleeping, and had asked me for nothing. "I'm awake," you said quietly—and turning to me, brought me home.

I could not look at you afterwards, Maggie, because there are times when happiness is close to pain . . . so I dressed, and drank the coffee that was still sitting by the window, and stood there watching the morning. "Do you want breakfast?" you asked. Yes, I said, but I think I'll take a walk first. I want to be alone. . . . "All right. I'll have breakfast ready when you come back." I walked to the door, still not looking at you, and went down to the street stricken by happiness that was like pain . . . and in love with you. I walked east, towards the river, and saw nothing but my happiness. The people going to work were my happiness, and the tenement buildings, and kids with their schoolbooks, and merchants opening their stores, and birds on the sidewalk and rainbow colors in the street. And I did not feel proud or vain, the way men are supposed to feel the first time—only humble—because you had given me back to myself. I had taken you, and found me . . . and though I could not understand it, it was happiness. I started to cry and leaned against a lamppost, but then I realized how crazy it was to be crying, so I stopped . . . and suddenly I wanted to buy something. Something beautiful for you. I had no money, so I thought I would pick flowers in the park. But there were no flowers in the park, so I walked farther east wondering what I could bring you. Capture a pigeon! Steal oranges from a pushcart! No, find pop bottles and get the deposit and *buy* an orange. One perfect orange . . . I kept walking, thinking of oranges, until I realized that I had turned around and was heading back to your place. Running. . . .

I burst in the door and you looked at me with tears in your eyes.

"Maggie? What's wrong—what is it?"

"I thought you weren't coming back."

"Oh, no! I just wanted to buy you something."

"I thought you'd never . . ."

"But I did. See? I came back. I wanted to buy you an orange. . . ."

Then we were holding each other, and kissing, and the puppy was barking and the coffee was boiling, and though you had cooked breakfast, we never ate it. . . . Oh, Maggie, those first hours with you . . . I cannot write them well enough . . . and then it was dark, soft darkness, with the puppy asleep at our feet.

"Maggie . . . have you been with many people?"

"Just one."

"I thought it was more."

"Why? Do I seem jaded?"

"No, no. You're beautiful. I just thought . . ."

"Don't think of these things. I'm with you now."

"You don't know me."

"Yes, David. I do."

"Isn't it funny? I feel the same way. Like we had grown up together or something. How old are you?"

"Nineteen."

"Oh . . . you're older than I am. Where are you from?"

"Boston. I went to school in New York, though."

"Do your parents know you're here?"

"My father does. My mother's in a sanitarium."

"How come?"

"Such a long story."

"Tell me . . ."

"Well, she's an alcoholic, so she goes to sanitariums. And then she comes out of sanitariums, and then she goes back in. Year after year."

"What about that organization?"

"Alcoholics Anonymous? She won't go. . . . Oh, David, how can I tell you my life so it'll make sense? It doesn't even make sense to me."

"Try."

"Well . . . my father always liked other women. So my mother drank. The fact that she was the cause of his infidelity never occurred to her. She's a complainer, never thinks anything is her fault, and she keeps threatening suicide. My brother Don left home very young—he's in England now—and I tried to run away when I was thirteen, only they caught me. I never liked living at home, that's all."

"Your father knows you're in New York?"

"Of course. He pays for this loft."

"And you let him?"

"Why not? He's glad to be rid of me. I take part-time jobs, though. It's not his fault—I was a rotten child. Selfish, mean, always wanting to be things I couldn't. That's the secret to me, David, I always wanted to *be* something. A writer, a painter, an actress. And I never had an ounce of talent. So I went to Sarah Lawrence to be a writer or a painter or an actress, and I wasn't any good, so I decided to be a hippie. And no one objected."

"Did you want them to?"

"Yes . . . I think I did. Sounds funny, doesn't it?"

"No."

"I always kept pushing limits, breaking rules, waiting for people to stop me. But after a while, nobody did. They just let me go."

"Do you want to go back?"

"Home? No, it's too late for that."

"It's the same with me."

"Your story now."

"Not yet. How long have you been down here?"

"Seven months, eight . . . I don't remember. I thought it was going to be wonderful—and then I met people like Cowboy. Quite a letdown. But I had nowhere else to go, so I stayed, and painted bad pictures and wrote bad poems and tried to keep people from raping me. And then I met a man . . . well, I thought I cared for him, but it was just loneliness. He was a dealer."

"So you took dope."

"Only twice. I hated it."

"Why?"

"Because it's death with colors, and I want to live. I may not be a very good person, but I do want to live."

"You are a good person, Maggie."

"I don't know that yet."

"You are very beautiful. . . . Did this guy hurt you badly?"

"Yes."

"And yet you made love with me. Why?"

"Because . . . because if you lose your faith, there's nothing left. And my faith is in people. You're sleepy, aren't you?"

"Yes."

"Then go to sleep and I'll hold you. Good-night, David."

"Maggie?"

"Yes?"

"Nothing. Good-night."

THERE'S SOMETHING VERY FUNNY about this. My whole life in a notebook—and underneath the words a blank. No clearer than when I started, no answers. What did I want? A blinding flash of revelation? Yes. After all, the only thing Buddha did was sit under a tree and POW! he was enlightened. Ah, but he was being rewarded for asceticism, whereas I smoke pot, drink beer, and make love. As often as possible. . . . I was thinking of Ben this morning—the question he asked me after the funeral. Lunch was over and the Lowensteins had gone home (Arnie drunk) when Ben came into the den and found me watching television. A soap opera. Mom was doing the dishes with Bessie, and the apartment seemed so strange and haunted that I wanted to take my mind off things. I looked up and saw him in the doorway.

You want me to turn off the set?

No, Davy. I don't mind.

I suppose you think it's sacrilegious.

Not at all. Some people drink after a funeral, others watch television. Just a way of letting down.

I see.

Davy, I want to ask you something . . .

OK. Ask.

What went wrong between you and Leo? I never knew.

It isn't important.

It is to me. He loved you very much.

Ben . . .

I know you don't want to talk about it. But it's bothered me for a long time. Was it connected with your friend? The one who died?

No. Just in the beginning.

Then what went wrong?

I don't know.

Your work? It's true that he didn't understand it . . .

Look—I don't know what went wrong. I thought it

was Rick, but it wasn't. Don't you see? The truth is that *I don't know.*

He thought I wasn't being honest, but to this day I don't know what happened—and I'd give ten years of my life to find the answer. The thing that hurt him was that we had never reconciled. To him, I was Absalom and Dad was King David: a biblical tragedy. But tragedy needs stature and neither of us had any . . . just two people fighting each other. Who won, Leo? It must have been you, because I want my life and you're still hanging onto it. . . . I felt sorry for Ben, sitting there watching the soap opera. He seemed so alone. And if I could have given him "a truth" I would have done so, wrapped up like a package with the strings tied. No truths. Just the memory of that night with Rick, when Leo finally revealed himself. Wow, as Marty would say. Too much. Because when you see a parent behave like that, you wonder: if he is like this, then what am *I?* If my own father is so cruel, so wrong, so vile, then who am I to have come from him? It still wasn't the cause, though. . . . I'll explain it to you, Benjamin—the minute I can explain it to myself.

Maggie . . . I want to write about you now, just the way it happened. I moved in with you the third day, despite Marty's protests. ("Who *is* this chick?" he kept asking. "You don't even know her. Does Cowboy know her? Who the hell *knows* her?" Marty, I said happily, you sound like somebody's mother.) So great . . . moving in my things and my paintings, Pablo barking and you laughing, and our clothes in the same closet, and a bigger bed to be bought. The newness of it: watching you cook meals and iron blouses and wash your hair. Watching you wake in the morning. So much talk and never enough time for talk, our words ending in kisses. . . . I couldn't get over it—that no matter where I went, I would come home to you. That I could go out for a whole day and return to a girl named Maggie Carroll from Boston. A girl who was truly beautiful. Who people looked at on the street. Who dressed in the colors I liked and didn't need makeup, and whose hair was softer than rain. . . . It's like the movies, I kept thinking. You fall in love and go out of your mind with happiness. You love bus drivers and strangers in the park, and every action, every small thing, is transformed. Food tastes better. And sleep is good. And you like your own looks again because she likes them, and you are at ease together, gentle and good as good children, and nothing in the world can hurt as badly as before because there are two of you. . . . You depended on me. Admired my work. Thought I was funny and kind. But it worked both ways, because you were strong where I was weak, and patient where I was not, and tolerant of things I wasn't. It was like we were two halves of a coin that had been split apart, and then put back together. And there were times when we made love . . . when truly we were not two people, but one living breathing thing. You loved me and so I loved myself again, the person I was and the person I would become. . . .

You know what I liked most about you? That you woke up happy. You, who had had the saddest life of anyone I'd known, woke up cheerful, kissed me, and took

Pablo out for a walk. Not bubbling, just happy—and patient with my moods. Silent and good when my work didn't go well, and overjoyed when it did. You knew that work was the secret to me, and you were honest about my work. Went to galleries and understood what you saw. Understood deeper than I did . . . because, Maggie, at nineteen you knew more than most people do at ninety. You, who said you had no talent for anything, had a talent I didn't—for life. You were good with people in stores, kind to bums who came up to you on the street . . . and beautiful with children. And if you had a temper, it only burst out when things were cruel and unjust, things you couldn't fix. You had a million imperfections. Smoked too much. Put yourself down in conversations. And had a terrible habit of talking to yourself—stern little lectures. You were so compulsively neat that it drove me crazy, and you loved rearranging the furniture (all six pieces of it). You believed in health foods and made me eat yogurt . . . but you were real, and you were mine, and that was the miracle.

I kept thinking of Rick, because we did things he would have liked. Discovering the Village, for example. Not just the East Village, but the West: The White Horse Tavern where Dylan Thomas had read his poems and gotten drunk. Patchin Place where E. E. Cummings had lived. Edna St. Vincent Millay's home, and the Provincetown Playhouse where Eugene O'Neill had worked, and coffee houses and antique stores and the dozens of thrift shops that we loved because the clothes were so great. We had $300.00 between us and spent it. Bought wonderful crazy outfits and hats and sandals and a whole library of secondhand books. You liked Judy Collins records and I bought you some. Then you gave me the poems of Anne Sexton. So I bought you Neruda and the poems of Leonard Cohen, and it went on and on, an endless birthday. . . . Pablo running ahead of us down Greenwich Avenue, picnics in Washington Square Park, the outdoor art show. I loved the way other guys smiled at you on the street (as long as you didn't smile back) and loved most of all coming home with you to kick off our shoes and lie down together, presents all over the floor. . . .

There was only one thing we disagreed about, and it started that day in the park. Pablo was chasing pigeons and we were sitting on the grass—you in a floppy hat and a wide skirt and the beads I had bought you. You looked so beautiful, but then you began talking about Leo.

"Do you think he'd like me?"

"No. He wouldn't let himself."

"Why?"

"Because . . . hell, I don't know. Because you're mine."

"I feel strange—not knowing him."

"Why? You're lucky to be out of it."

"He's your father, David."

"Oh, honey, you sound like my Uncle Benjamin."

"I'd like to know him, too. All of them."

"That's so corny."

"Well, I am corny. Beneath this exterior is a very square girl. A believer in families. . . . Don't worry, I'm not proposing."

"Go ahead. Propose."

"What would you say if I did?"

"What would you say if *I* did?"

"No."

"Oh . . . how come?"

"We're not ready yet. Did you love him when you were little?"

"Yes, but *why* do we have to talk about it?"

"Because he haunts you. Don't look at me that way —he does. It's so sad. Here's this man eating his heart out, and you won't even phone him."

"Look who's talking!"

"My father doesn't want me. Yours does."

"What would you like me to do? Rush up to Riverside Drive and throw my arms around him? Burst into hot, penitent tears?"

"No, I just want you to make peace with him. Because if you don't, it will always bother you. It's you I care about."

"Doesn't sound like it."

"God, you're spoiled."

"Kiss me."

"Here?"

"Sure. Everyone kisses in parks."

"Not me."

"You're the most confusing girl I've ever known. The minute I think you're wild, you turn out to be conventional. And the minute I think . . ."

"That's why you like me. David, aren't you ever going to tell him about me?"

"Look, it's a beautiful day, and we're eating fresh roasted peanuts, and I worship you. I would even die for you. But as far as my father is concerned, nothing doing."

"I think you still love him."

"Wrong."

"And I also think you're afraid of loving him."

"Well, *I* think you never should have studied Psychology at Sarah Lawrence. It messed your head up. Come on. Kiss me."

"Not in the park."

"You kiss me at home . . ."

"That's different. Home is private."

"Maggie, will you marry me someday? I want to."

"You don't have to say that."

"I know, but I can't imagine loving anyone else. You're the only person I want."

"Because I'm the first."

"You think I'll change?"

"You might."

"Impossible. We're perfect together."

"We're not even twenty, David, and divorce scares me. My brother's been divorced and he's only twenty-eight. Two children, and his whole life spent supporting them. He doesn't even see them, just sends a check every month."

"Aren't you sure of me?"

"Yes, but you aren't sure of yourself."

"How?"

"Your relationship with your father . . ."

"God, you make me mad."

"I'm sorry."

"Stop saying you're *sorry* about everything. My father has nothing to do with us—and if you don't want to marry me, then to hell with it. We'll live in sin."

We began to laugh because the expression was so

old-fashioned, but the trouble had begun. And as the days passed, the subject of Leo became a tense thing between us. I couldn't figure it out because no matter what you said, Maggie, you were not a conventional person. . . . We had our first argument and I walked out on you. Came back, and left again. I loved you better than life, better than myself . . . yet by autumn I was yelling at you, and walking out, and coming back to apologize. I became critical of you—your looks, your habits—and then wanted to kill myself. Came into the house with a present for you, and started all over again. It was Leo I was angry at, not you, but I couldn't have known that—so I hurt you over and over, saying things I didn't mean. Any other girl would have left, but there was something in you . . . so good, so honest, that you wouldn't do it. You stayed. Through tears and through arguments. Through days when I wouldn't say a word and nights when all I wanted was love. You stayed with me. . . .

I'm getting mixed up, things in the wrong sequence, because Dad found out about Maggie in July. He and Mom had been away on vacation, but when they got back they learned that I had moved. Leo phoned at once, and it was not what you would call a friendly conversation. The amazing thing was that he started right in on me. We hadn't spoken for months, yet to hear him on the phone you would have thought it was yesterday. The same old crap. Authority, demands, power politics.

OK, mister. I've talked to your friend Marty and I know the whole story. And believe me, I'm pretty shocked. I don't shock easy, but this is the worst.

Dad, wait a minute . . .

(*161*)

What kind of family does a girl come from that she should live openly with a young man, not even being engaged? You think it's smart to live like that?

Dad, listen . . .

No, mister, you listen to *me*. Because this thing is gonna destroy your mother, and if you don't care about her, then you have no feelings. You said you couldn't live at home, so we let you go. It almost killed us. No college, no future, nothing. But we let you go. So how do you repay us? By picking up some . . .

You're not going to say that!

By picking up some cheap girl and moving in with her. Marty, I approved of, even if it was a bad neighborhood. But now where do I find you? With some tramp.

I'm going to hang up on you! I mean it.

You hang up and I'm sending the cops down there. I must have been crazy—letting you have your own way. What does a teen-age boy know about anything? You know the trouble you can get into? The diseases?

Dad, shut up. I'm sorry, but just shut up for a minute. Her name is Maggie Carroll and she's from Boston, and her father is a research scientist.

So tell me what she's doing in that apartment with you.

We love each other.

Love? Don't make me laugh. You can't even love your own people.

My own what?

Your own family, your own kind. What is this girl? Irish?

Oh, God, are you going to pull a *Jewish* thing on me? I mean, that's really too much.

Well, you're living with this girl . . .

And you don't know her, so I'm supposed to feel guilty. Right?

I made a bad mistake with you, Davy. Giving in to you, trying to please you. I listened to everyone but myself. But now I'm coming down there.

OK. But the minute you get me home, I'm leaving again. And if you lock me up, I'll jump out the window. And every time you bring me back I'll leave. Because what you can't understand is that I don't want to live with you. I don't even like you.

What did you say?

I said I don't like you as a human being.

Well, that's too goddamn bad about you! I'm your father and I have rights!

You have no rights.

I have rights! And no teen-age child is going to talk to me this way. I'll get a lawyer . . .

You do that.

And I'll take this case to court!

Fine.

And you'll be sorry for every mean thing, every cruel thing you have done to us! What did we do that you should hate us this way? You tell me what we did that was so terrible. We loved you! That was a terrible thing? And we gave to you from our hearts . . .

There was a silence. Then Mom got on the phone.

David, your father can't talk anymore. He's too upset.

Well, so am I.

I know that, darling, but there's going to come a point when you'll have to see him and straighten things out. He can't go on this way much longer.

Neither can I—only nobody thinks about that! Why doesn't anybody care what *I* feel? No matter what I do, it's wrong. I could be living in the suburbs with two Cadillacs and five children and it still wouldn't be any good. He's got it in for me, can't you see that?

That's not true, Davy.

It is true! He's had it in for me ever since Rick. And why? Because he was losing his hold on me and his ego couldn't take it. . . .

Oh, to hell with it. Write something happy for a change. Something funny. This whole thing's turning into a soap opera. . . . OK. Here's a joke: The Old Woman Who Lives In A Shoe is sitting in her enormous shoe, looking out at all the other shoes. Modern, split-level shoes, with swimming pools in back. Her neighbor, Mrs. Mandelbaum, comes over for a visit and they go into the kitchen for a cup of coffee. "So how are things?" asks Mrs. Mandelbaum. "Terrible," says the Old Woman, "terrible. I wouldn't bore you with it."

"You're lonely?" "It's not important. I don't sleep, I don't eat, and the only person I talk to is the canary— but it's not important." "Rose," says Mrs. Mandelbaum, "this is no life for you. Your son the doctor has grown up and moved to New York, and your son the lawyer is in Miami. Your daughter who made the good marriage is in California. And your husband, God bless him, passed away two years ago. Why don't you do yourself a favor? Move into a sandal."

Well, I thought it was funny when Chester told it to me, but I must have been stoned. . . . Poor old Chester. I saw him on the street last month and he hadn't changed. Still the water rat with little beady eyes. He was cool at first because of my defection, but after a while he warmed up and told me about the family. Valiant had been busted for selling pot-brownies to kids, and two days later everyone had split: Cowboy and Happy to some commune out west, Tiny and Dormouse back to the Haight, Preacher to Bellevue for observation. Only Chester was left, panhandling and sleeping in the park. "I haven't been stoned for a week," he said sadly. I gave him a few bucks and watched him stumble away . . . and then I started thinking about the fact that I wasn't using acid anymore. Pot had become natural to me, a form of relaxation, but the rest. . . . There had been one perfect trip and it had done something beautiful to my work. But after that I had grown disoriented, seeing too many levels of reality. How to hold a brush when your hand has a thousand fingers? How to mix colors when you are sealed inside a glass envelope? That last vision was so awful—me, Leo and Mom, floating in a crystal fluid, glass ropes tying us to each other. . . . But acid isn't a crime against the self, as Ben once said. More like a sacrament, to be used with faith. Maggie doesn't agree, but I know that future religions will be based on the use of psychedelics. Because Jesus and Buddha and Mohammed just didn't have a sense of color. . . .

In autumn we had been together for six months. This was a landmark, considering the fights we'd had, so we celebrated with wine and flowers and a soup bone for Pablo. I loved you so much that night, Maggie, watching you set the table—and suddenly I made a promise to myself to become the person you wanted. Half the time you took care of me, and the other half I treated you badly. Yet I loved you better than anyone. . . . We sat down and you reached across the table and took my hand.

"Happy anniversary, David."

"It's great, isn't it? Six months."

"Did you think it would last this long?"

"Yes."

"I didn't."

"Why?"

"Because you've been so unhappy."

"Not with you."

"Is your work all right?"

"No, nothing's all right . . . I wish you didn't have a job. I miss you during the day."

"But it's so easy, showing paintings to people."

"Is Morris still chasing after you?"

"No. The gallery keeps him too busy."

"I go crazy sometimes, thinking of him trying to make you. All the galleries in the Village, and you had to choose one owned by a sex maniac."

"I can take care of myself. David . . . I have an anniversary present for you."

"Oh. I didn't get you anything."

"That doesn't matter, but I'm afraid you'll be mad at me."

"Why? What have you done?"

"Promise you won't get mad?"

"Sure."

"Well, I took three of your paintings over to Morris yesterday. And he wants to give you a show."

"You're kidding! A one-man show?"

"Yes. If you can have enough work done by December."

"Fantastic! What pictures did he see?"

"The one of Dormouse, and the one of me, and . . ."

"Hey, wait a minute. Why is he doing this?"

"Because he liked your work."

"Does it have anything to do with you?"

"Of course not."

"How do I know that? How do I know he isn't using this as a way to . . ."

"Oh, David."

"Well, how do I know he isn't? The guy's got a thing for you. Anyone can see that."

"I don't understand. Every time something good happens, you try to spoil it. What are you afraid of?"

"Nothing! But if I wanted a show, I would have gotten one for myself. Stop being my mother."

"I don't want to be your mother. You insist on it."

"I'm sorry."

"Let's change the subject."

"Maggie . . . something's all wrong. I thought love fixed everything, but it doesn't."

"Be honest. You thought *sex* fixed everything."

"Sex and love—they're the same with us."

"You have to love yourself."

"That isn't the answer."

"It is with you. You're so ambivalent. And it hurts me, because Morris looked at your work and couldn't believe you were nineteen. He was terribly impressed."

"Funny. Rick said that too."

"What?"

"That I was ambivalent about my painting. I don't know . . . it must be my father. He was always so critical of my stuff."

"Because he felt rejected. You can't have it both ways—pushing him out, then wanting his approval."

"It's our anniversary and we're fighting."

"No, *you're* fighting. I don't have anything to fight about."

"Honey, please forgive me. I'll do the show. Please . . . love me."

You came over and kissed me, and for a moment everything was all right—but something was eating me that I couldn't understand. I had thought that freedom and love were the answer, that those two things would make me whole. But I was still trapped, guilty about Leo and furious at the guilt. . . . How do you get rid of people? Sometimes when I smoke pot, or sleep all day, I feel him looking down at me with a vast and holy disapproval. The dead don't die at all. They just become silent watchmen.

My show . . . a sudden goal, an excitement, a new happiness. I worked like a madman, ten hours a day. I wasn't frightened anymore, took chances, and Morris dropped in a few times to see the work and said all the right things. I didn't even care if the show was successful. The only thing that mattered was this sea of discovery— the canvases getting larger and larger, the colors bold. . . . Just one setback, but it almost finished me: Mom inviting us to supper. Why did I go? Because I was accomplishing something and felt I could face Dad again. Because I had a new pride in myself. Because . . . I had Maggie. We spent three hours getting ready, and bought a bottle of wine, and all the way up on the subway I felt a tremendous anticipation, imagining Leo's face when he saw her. I knew that she would be good with him, that he would like her despite himself . . . and then he didn't show up. Delayed at the office. His place at the table empty. Mom was surprised by Maggie, liked her at once, but the pain in me was so great . . . I couldn't understand why it hurt so much after a year and a half, but I could hardly speak that night. And *it doesn't matter* what his reasons were. So cruel. But it made me realize that my hatred was justified. He had been screaming over the phone for a year and a half, complaining that

I wouldn't see him, and then he chickened out. . . .

December 5th, four o'clock, and to my amazement dozens of people were walking into Morris Weidman's little gallery, and introducing themselves to me, and looking at my work. Not hippies, but uptown people. Amazing. Women in fur coats, men roaming around with punch glasses in their hands—and red stars going on some of the pictures. Sold. Sold. I couldn't believe it, so I just stood in a corner, watching. . . . Maggie was hostess and she looked beautiful: velvet slacks with bell-bottoms, and a satin blouse. After an hour the door opened and Mom and Benjamin came in. Without Leo. And though I'd been prepared for that, it gave me a bad moment. Then I introduced Benjamin to Maggie and his face lit up. I knew that Dad had told him I was living with some tramp, and now he was meeting the loveliest girl in the world whose manners were pure finishing school. He acted like an adolescent with her, and wound up buying one of her portraits. So it was victory—of many kinds. The funny thing was the questions people asked me. With straight faces. Are you a Process Painter? Do you ever work with environments? I think Super Realism is divine, don't you? Is the figure coming back, or do you think it's passé? I said yes to everything and had a rough time not laughing—but in a strange way it didn't matter that so many of them were phonies, because something was getting through.

A week later reviews came out in a couple of the Village papers, and they were so good that Maggie and I were overwhelmed. We bought up whole newsstands, like actors on opening night, and pasted the articles in a scrapbook. I don't know why, but I would have given anything for Dad to see them. The same old need to prove myself, I guess, but I had to stop myself from sending him copies. The hardest thing I ever did.

A stifling summer. Half the time I can't sleep. Drink iced tea in the kitchen, lie in the bathtub and read. Watch Maggie sleep like a child, one arm across her face. . . . The longest summer of my life. Work going badly and hours spent wandering the streets. A displaced person. No, a displaced artist, writing instead of painting. . . . Last night I wrote a poem for Rick.

> *Poised between childhood and age*
> *He has been snared unwittingly,*
> *His sudden flash of light*
> *Easy for the net's capture.*
> *Imprisoned, he does not know his plight*
> *But swims into the net as to a sea.*
>
> *He is seeking distances; an upper air*
> *Through which his mind may roll.*
> *Skimming sun from off the sky's pure bowl*
> *This net might be eternity, no prison*
> *But a catch of light.*
>
> *Not seeing that a field of trees*
> *Has made a cage; blinded to the heart's*
> *Dark penalties, he waits.*
> *And he is singing, close within the bars,*
> *Unknowing that from out the simplest air*
> *His song was ripped*
> *And fell among the stars.*

A few words in return for a lifetime. A poem to replace a friend who deserted him. Who judged him. Who didn't even weep when he died, just got drunk. . . . I can't make it up to him. Death is too final.

But I *can* tell the truth. What in the name of God is this story for, if not truth! I've avoided that incident for weeks, writing around it, circling it like an animal, alluding to it because I was afraid to put it on paper. Tell the truth! Because really, really, really—nothing worse will ever happen to me.

Benjamin, you wondered what took place that night. Here it is.

Scene: a warm night in May, my parents at a party, and Rick and I reading in my room. Defying Dad, yet planning to leave before he comes home. Time: nine o'clock. Vibrations: excellent. I am at the desk while he lies on the bed, smoking, humming, flipping pages of books. We have not spoken for an hour, but there is harmony between us tonight, a certain peace, as though we have both decided that things will work out. (These hours and minutes are painted on my mind, and I can remember the shirt he was wearing and the hole in his shoe, and the way his hair fell down hiding his eyes.) Misty night, warm spring, a few raindrops. And it seems to me that we have been friends for a hundred years, and that nothing can hurt us or happen to us because we are at peace together. No suspicions or criticisms. He accepts the squareness of me as I accept the difference of him, and for a little time, this night only, the world seems good. . . . With a sudden twist of mood he rolls off the bed and starts to laugh. Laughing for no reason at all, but infectious laughter, so that I join him. Then we are hors-

ing around, sparring, doing an Indian war dance, everything getting sillier by the moment. He does an imitation
of Chaplin, his hero, and it is very funny. I push him and
he topples over. "You're too flabby!" I yell, imitating
Dad. "Why don't you take more sports? What kind of all-
American kid are you?" We are wrestling now, trying to
see who is stronger—and panting we crash to the floor.
Give up? he asks. "No!" I shout, and try to pin his arms
behind him. He gets the better of me and straddles me,
forcing me down. Still we are laughing, amazed to find
ourselves doing something so classically youthful.
Pleased, almost, to find ourselves wrestling like two characters out of a turn-of-the-century boys' book. It occurs
to me that I will probably hurt my back again, so I laugh
all the harder. And his laughter is filling the room like
wonderful crazy music, his yellow hair swinging over his
eyes. There is a crash. The door has burst open. It is
. . . I don't know. Someone has kicked open the door.
It. . . . Someone is pulling Rick off me, his face contorted. Someone is. . . . Yes—Leo. But like a madman,
pulling Rick off, yanking him away by the collar. But
. . . why? "OK, sonny, that's it, that's all, everything's
over. Now, out! Out of this house!" It is happening too
fast. My father is dragging Rick into the hall and his
voice is murderous. He's hurting him! I run down the
hall, and Leo has backed Rick up against a table, his fist
clutching Rick's collar, his face white with a rage I do
not understand and cannot believe. *What is the matter
with him?*

"Take your hands off me!" says Rick. "I mean it,
Mr. Marks!"

"I'll take them off when I hear that you're never

coming in this house again. I want to hear it from your mouth."

"You're hurting me!"

"What's the matter—you don't like it? I thought creeps like you liked being roughed up. Only this is a decent home, and my son is a decent boy!"

"I don't know what you're talking about!"

"Oh, yes you do. You lousy little *queer* . . ."

I tore Leo's hands away and Rick ran out the door. Then I looked at this man, my father, this man from whom I had come, the reason for my existence on earth —looked at him as squarely as I have ever looked at anyone—and went to my room to pack.

I could not take them in, the words Leo had used, so they hovered above me like birds over a carcass . . . I was dead now, as I went to school and lived at Marty's and did my homework and saw Rick—allied with him yet unable to discuss what had happened. The words stood between us like a third person. We laughed and they returned. I put my hand on his arm and he pulled away. From the words. We would glance at each other in class, only to see—the words. And the fact that they were not true did not help us. Perhaps the words were the reason he went away that summer and gave in to his father's demands and joined the army. It is possible that the words helped to kill him, as he went off to be a MAN in capital letters, manhood being violence in this culture. Everything is possible, but . . .

And if the words were true.

What then?

Nothing, no different. No different, I swear. Love is

color-blind and sex-blind and age-blind. Has to be, or it makes no sense. Why guilt over what we are? Why *my* guilt? Because of you, Leo, only because of you. I came into this world unharmed, clean, open to love—and you changed me. . . . I can't lie anymore, saying that the incident ruined my life, made me leave home, got me hung-up on drugs. Our trouble started long before Rick Heaton and survives him. I just feel a sadness tonight, realizing that you lived to be fifty-five years old without knowing who I was, without looking at me. I'm not so terrible, you know, even if I did have those dirty, abnormal, effeminate feelings. I am actually in some ways . . . beautiful. And if the child is father to the man, then let me instruct you. Let me stand over your grave and give you a final lesson: real love is a gift, and those lucky enough to get it even once in life are special. I have been very lucky because two people have loved me more than I deserve, and I never repaid them with anything more than need. My need to be taken care of. This is a miserable thing but I can't change it, because whatever I am, you created. The fears, the doubts, the insecurities—these are your gifts, Leo—and you will forgive me if I don't say thank you. The one miracle is that I am human at all.

I had such dreams after my show . . . of making a living with my work and marrying Maggie. Of going to Europe. Of being happy. . . . A new quietness between Maggie and me, friends coming into our lives, kids who lived in the building. Spaghetti parties with wine, and a boy named Michael playing the guitar and a girl named Joanna singing. Our best friend, Lincoln Smith, telling stories about the south and his great-grandparents who had been slaves, and how four men had tried to kill him for sitting in a white restaurant when he was sixteen. A beautiful man who didn't care about black power or white power, politics or presidents. When I asked him why, he smiled. "Son, before you change the world, you have to change yourself." And I never forgot that.

Spring came again and we were happy, Lincoln taking his meals with us, Pablo growing into an enormous hound dog, a few people commissioning pictures from me. Our life had almost become what we wanted. . . . And then it happened—the end or the beginning—I still don't know which.

It was Maggie who answered the phone, and as she spoke to my mother a strange look passed over her face. "I'm so sorry," she said. "Let me get David." Then I was talking to Mom and learning that Leo had to have an operation. Gall stones, a lot of pain, going into the hospital next week . . . I didn't feel much about it, but said I was sorry, and was about to hang up when her voice got tense.

Aren't you going to visit him in the hospital?

No. Why should I?

Why *should* you? Because he's your father.

Mom, please don't start this again. I'm sorry he's having an operation, but I can't do anything about it.

You can go to the hospital.

Let his friends go.

He doesn't have any friends—he's alienated all of them.

Because of me, I suppose.

Yes, because of you. He's been impossible this year, insulting people, losing customers. The only person who will see him is Arnie Lowenstein.

Then let Arnie go.

David, I'm asking you to do one thing . . .

Well, I'm refusing! Look—fair is fair. I came to dinner, he stayed at the office. I had my own show, he stayed home. What do you want me to do? Forget about that?

No, I just want you to find a little charity inside yourself. He's been sick for months and wouldn't see a doctor. Now I don't know what they'll find.

You said it was gall stones.

That's what they think it is, but . . .

Then stop worrying so much. I'll call you next week. OK? I have to go now.

Maggie said I was wrong, but I could no more have gone to that hospital than . . . what? Loved him again, I suppose. I just didn't feel responsible. Or concerned. And if it was heartless, then it was heartless. But gall stones . . . Marty's father had had the same thing and it was nothing. The day after the operation I called Mom and couldn't reach her. Called Ben too, but no luck. So I figured they'd call me—only they didn't. I waited for two days, and had just decided to phone the hospital when someone knocked on the door. I opened it and got a shock—because it was Mom. Maggie had gone to the store for some milk, and I wasn't dressed yet.

"Mom? Is anything. . . . Wait. I'll put some clothes on."

"You can stay in your bathrobe, David. I want to talk to you."

"OK. Would you like a cup of coffee?"

"No."

"Well . . . how is he?"

"He's very sick. And I want you to go and see him."

"I can't do that."

"I want you to go over there, and visit him, and show some concern."

"Was the operation a success?"

"No."

"Why are you looking at me that way? What's wrong?"

"He has cancer."

"Oh. God, I'm sorry. And they didn't know it?"

"Not till they operated."

"That's terrible. But what good would it do for me . . ."

"What good! You can sit there and ask what *good* it would do to see him? The man has cancer!"

"I know—and I'm sorry. Truly. But it's too late for him and me. The relationship was finished a long time ago."

"No relationship is ever finished. It only takes one person to . . ."

"Can't you see how phony it would be for me to go

to that hospital? Pretending that nothing had happened? I can't lie to him."

"Why not? What's so noble about you that you can't lie?"

"Don't start this again. Please."

"I will start it! There has to come a point in your life when you're willing to do something for another person. *That* is adulthood, my dear, not living in the Village with a girl."

"Keep Maggie out of this."

"I will say what I feel! Because that man is sick, and you owe him something. Maybe he wasn't a perfect father, but no one is perfect. All he ever cared about was you. And how did you repay him? With insults, with cruelty, ignoring him for two years. Well, he's human and so he was hurt and didn't come to your show."

"You don't even know him . . ."

"All you see in your father is what you *want* to see. You criticized him and criticized him, yet you took his money, took everything he gave you. That isn't my idea of independence. If you hate someone, you shouldn't live off them."

"Forgive me, Mother, but that's a lot of crap. I was a child when I took those things."

"David, I'm going to say something I thought I'd never say to you—because you're my son and I love you —but you are a spoiled, selfish person who has never given a thought to anyone but himself. You think you're a man now because you're living with Maggie. All right, times have changed. In my day, young people didn't do such things. But freedom and sex don't mean maturity!

(*179*)

You wonder why your father is so difficult. Well, you were the only thing in the world he loved—yes, better than he loved me—and you shut him out. With your snobbery, with your phony intellectualism, with your friends. From the time you were a little boy, you made him feel that you were ashamed of him. And what do you think that does to a man?"

"I didn't raise myself! It was he who sent me to that school and dressed me like something out of an English novel. Summer camp, tennis lessons . . ."

"Your father didn't have enough to eat as a child, and you wonder why he wanted a better life for you!"

"It kills me for you to talk this way—because *you don't know him.*"

"I know this man, and I love this man! He isn't perfect, and if you're talking about other women, I know all about that. And about his business dealings! And about the fact that he's ashamed of being a Jew! I know these things and forgive them, because Leo Marks is a *man*—more of a man than you'll ever be—and I'm proud of him. He has guts and he has goodness, and if he's made mistakes, they're human mistakes and should be forgiven. Only *you* can't forgive him. Only you."

"Please, Mom . . ."

"So what I'm ordering you to do, is to go to that hospital and tell your father you love him—even if you don't mean it. Because he's dying."

"He's . . ."

"He has cancer and he's dying."

"Does . . . does he know it?"

"Yes. He asked the doctors for the truth, and they told him."

"How long can he live?"

"Nobody knows that."

"Well, aren't they *doing* anything for him?"

"He'll have cobalt treatments."

"That's all?"

"Of course it isn't all! He'll have every treatment they've invented. And his money, that you hate so much, will make it possible."

"God. I'm so sorry."

"Then show it! Act like an adult for a change."

"But . . ."

"Just be at that hospital tomorrow. He's on the fourth floor, and I want you to look decent when you see him. I'm going home now, because I have a lot of thinking to do. I don't know how I'm going to live without him, or how I can bear it, but I'm going to see this thing through and be cheerful for him. And I expect you to do the same."

She turned and walked out the door—and I stood there as though she had hit me. I had never seen her like that, not once in my life, and it left me with a feeling that was . . . I can't describe it. She was so different, like a stranger, and the things she had said were impossible to understand. As though I didn't matter to her anymore, as though she didn't even love me . . . I couldn't sleep that night, thoughts going through my head like an express train. He was dying and we'd never made up. No more chances. Yes, there were. I could go to the hospital and resolve the thing, make peace with him. Because if I didn't . . . I lay there in the dark, holding Maggie's hand as she slept, and tried to remember when the trouble had started. Being little and loving him . . . being proud when he came to school . . . growing older and admiring him . . . the ball games we went to. He knew more about baseball than anyone in the world. Thinking he was important—then realizing that he wasn't. That he was just a little man who wanted to impress people. But still loving him . . . for a long time. Things crumbling slowly, a word here, an argument there, sudden criticisms. It couldn't have been my fault because I was only a child—so it must have been his . . . Yet what did it matter, now that he was dying? I would sit in the bleachers all afternoon but never felt the excitement he did, his face intense and happy. . . . "From the time you were a little boy, you made him feel that you were ashamed of him." Not true. I thought he was God. Would write down the name of every baseball player, wanting to like the game, wanting to be a companion to him, his kind of person. But the more he'd try to include me, the more he'd shut me out. I couldn't like the game as much as he did, his enthusiasm turned me cold. . . . How much of it was my fault? The years get blurred and I can't remember. . . . No answers. And now it's too late.

I got up at seven the next morning and put on clean clothes and a new pair of sandals. No beads, though I usually wore them . . . and then I thought of going to a barber. I knew Dad wouldn't like the long hair, but the idea of cutting it . . . well, I couldn't, and that was that. I held Maggie close to me for a moment and went down the stairs. Took a cab uptown for the first time in years, tipped the driver too much, and stood on the corner of York Avenue looking at the hospital. It occurred to me that I should bring him something, so I walked until I found a drugstore. Went in and bought two paperbacks —mysteries, which he used to like. Then I was entering the hospital and riding up in the elevator, more nervous than I'd ever been in my life.

I stood in the hall for a while to compose myself, and then I opened his door. A large room, lots of flowers, some books, a breakfast tray. . . .

"Dad?"

"Well. So you got here, huh?"

"Yes."

"Come in . . ."

"Thanks."

He was at least twenty pounds thinner, and it gave me a shock. No color in his face.

"How are you feeling?"

"Pretty good. You have any trouble finding the hospital?"

"No. I took a cab."

He wasn't looking at me, just arranging the things on his night table. And though I'd planned to kiss him, I couldn't.

"How's the weather outside?"

"Very nice. Warm."

"They have air conditioning here, but they haven't turned it on yet."

I couldn't think of anything to say, so I sat down near the window. He was arranging books on the night table. Then he poured himself a glass of water.

"Your mother said you were coming. . . . She told you I had a malignancy?"

"Yes."

"Well, it's nothing to worry about. Just a tumor, but they got it. I'll be home in a few weeks."

"Do you have any pain?"

"No, no. They give you shots for the pain. As far as I'm concerned, this is a vacation. A needed rest."

"Sure."

We fell silent, and I could hear the clock ticking on the bureau. A boat on the river. A plane.

"So what's the news? Seen Marty?"

"No. Not recently."

"I'm surprised. Two boyhood friends and they don't see each other. I always liked Marty."

He looked at me—for the first time—and tears came into his eyes. I stared out the window.

"How have you been, Davy?"

"Fine. Busy."

"You've changed."

"I know."

"This . . . this person you're staying with. She feeds you?"

"Of course."

"Doesn't look like it. You get any protein?"

"Yes."

"A few more pounds wouldn't hurt. A boy your age should look healthy."

"I'm fine. Really."

"This place you're staying in—it's got heat?"

I could feel the anger rising in me, but I stifled it. Please, I kept praying, just let this one visit go well. Let me do what I came here to do.

"Yes. Heat and hot water."

"In that neighborhood, I'm not so sure."

"Dad . . . tell me about yourself. Do you like your doctor?"

"Sure I like him. The top man in the country. He operated on one of the Kennedys."

"He must be very good then."

"You know your old man—only the best. But it worries me to see you so thin. Why don't you take a vacation? All work and no play isn't a good thing."

"Well, maybe this summer . . ."

"You know what I was thinking before you came? Here I am, stuck in the hospital, and there's our place in Florida sitting empty. Would you like to go down for a few weeks?"

"That would be nice. I'm kind of busy, though."

"Busy! Nineteen years old and he's busy. Come to my office and you'll see what it is to be busy. I didn't get home for supper one night last week. . . . How are you fixed for money?"

"I'm making some money with my work."

"You need a little extra?"

"No."

"What about clothes?"

"I've got everything I need. Really."

He reached in the drawer of the table, took out some mints, and offered me one. I shook my head.

"My mouth gets dry."

"Do they give you good service here?"

"Very good. The food, though, they could improve. You ever see your uncle?"

"Sometimes."

"Phone him occasionally. He's a lonely person."

"OK. I will."

"Two years is a long time. You're much taller—you know that? When you walked in the door, I didn't know who it was."

"Would you like me to raise the bed? You don't look comfortable."

"That would be nice. Turn the handle to the left."

"Better?"

"Yes, thanks. They don't let me move around much, so my back gets sore. The *schvartzeh* rubs it at night."

I bristled at the word, but tried not to show it. Keep quiet, I told myself. Let him say *schvartzeh* and *nigger* and anything he wants.

"You'll be twenty in the fall. Pretty grown-up. Got any plans?"

"For what?"

"For the future. What have you got in mind?"

"Nothing much."

"Come on, now. You always used to be full of plans."

I couldn't talk to him. He was looking at me so hungrily . . . it turned me cold.

"I guess I'll stay in the Village."

"And that's your idea of a great life?"

"Yes. It is."

"What happens when you're thirty?"

"I don't know. I haven't thought that far ahead."

"Do me a favor and think about it. When you're young, life seems very long. But it isn't. Time catches up with you."

He turned his head away, trying to control himself, and I thought: go over to him, kiss him, say something kind. Just this once, say something kind.

"I have to be going now, Dad."

"Really? You've only been here a few minutes."

"I have an appointment."

"Oh. That's too bad. . . . Listen, I saved a piece of pound cake for you."

"Pound cake?"

"Sure. Remember the way you used to love pound cake? They brought some for dessert last night, so I wrapped it in wax paper. Right over there."

"Thank you."

"Maybe you'll come next week."

"All right."

"The morning's the best time because I feel stronger then. Tuesday, maybe?"

"I'll be here."

"Good. But listen . . . before you come, get a haircut. I want the nurses to see you looking nice."

"The *nurses?*"

"And wear your other clothes. You know, a tie or something. The people around here are very high class."

"What does that have to do with . . ."

"A tie and a jacket. Just this once."

"OK."

"And a good haircut. Take some money from my wallet."

"I can pay for it myself."

"No, this time I'll pay. I want to be sure that . . ."

"I said, I'll pay for it myself!"

"Why the anger?"

"Let it alone, Dad."

"I just don't want you looking peculiar, that's all. Somebody might come in the room."

"Jesus."

"Don't swear at me."

"You know something? Where I live, ties and jackets are peculiar. It's all a matter of opinion."

"This is my room, and *my* opinion is that you look peculiar. I've told these people about you, and I want you to look nice."

"Do clothes make me nice?"

"I don't want an argument, Davy."

"Neither do I. But these clothes are a part of me. And I like my hair! And I'm proud of the way I look!"

Stop it, I told myself. In the name of God, stop it. The man is sick. He's dying.

"I don't want you back here until you can dress normal."

"Fine. Then I won't come back."

"But if you think this is being grown-up, you have a lot to learn. Only a child would act this way. I ask you to do one little thing . . ."

"It isn't little to me!"

"And you refuse. So stay away. Go back to that slum you live in."

"Look—I came here and tried to be nice . . ."

"Big deal! Once in two years."

"And you wouldn't let me. I tried to . . ."

"You don't know the meaning of the word try! All you know is yourself. Anyone else could starve as far as you're concerned. Is it my fault—this attitude? Because if it is, then I'm sorry for everything I gave you. All my life I worked hard for you, and what do I get in return? A person who can't even be polite! Who can't even be human! You give a child every advantage, and he turns into a bum. So you explain it to me."

"I don't want to fight with you, Dad."

"Then go away. Go back to your friends in the Village."

He started to cry as I left the room, but I didn't turn around. Just took the elevator down to the street and stood there, numb, distant. I walked downtown with the piece of cake in my hand, not seeing anything—and I must have gone ten blocks before I realized that the books were still in my pocket. The present I had bought him.

(He lay there for weeks and you didn't go back. Didn't phone to see how he was, didn't send a card or a flower. The conventional things, the right things, and you didn't do them. You felt like you didn't exist, like you were a figment of your own imagination. Anyone who was real would have been at the hospital, easing that man's death. No, you can't ease death. All you can do is sit there, make small talk, bring gifts. Pretend it isn't happening. Pretend a miracle will occur. Everyone does those things because they're the right things, so perhaps you were the monster they thought you were. Day after day passed, week after week . . . and you didn't go.)

There's no explaining it. I couldn't. Even though Mom wrote a bitter letter and Ben wrote a kind one—asking me to come because Leo's condition was worse.

The cancer had spread, and cobalt treatments hadn't helped. Chemotherapy hadn't helped. And he had private nurses now. . . . It wasn't anger, or holding a grudge, or being sadistic. More like—amnesia. I forgot about it and woke with nightmares. I tried to paint but never finished anything. I went to parties in the building and left after an hour. Walked the streets with my dog. . . . Stopped once, seeing my reflection in a window, and thought: this is what hurt him, the clothes, the hair, the sandals. The face that isn't shaved. The eyes with circles under them. This is what bothered him, not you but your exterior. Why can't you change that exterior, play a part, be someone else for a day? Why can't you do one last thing for him? Somewhere in the depths of you, you love him. No—it's guilt. Yes and no. Christ. You *are* the monster they think you are. Let them think it. Let them think anything they want. It isn't your fault, none of it. It just isn't your fault.

I sat on the edge of the bed, and Maggie woke up.

David . . .

Go back to sleep—I'm all right.

No, you're not.

I can't talk about it anymore.

We *have* to talk about it. He's going to die.

Everything you say is like Mom and Ben. You don't help me.

Why won't you see him?

He doesn't want me the way I am—and I can't change.

It's only a matter of clothes . . .

Well, why does he care so much about clothes?

Why do you?

Leave me alone, Maggie. Please.

I can't stand to see you hurting this way. What are you afraid of?

The minute I do what he wants I'm a little boy again, crippled.

You're crippled right now—and you haven't even seen him.

Don't you understand? The minute I go back to that hospital I'm his son again, his possession. And I can't take it!

If you'd only face him, the fear would go away. You have to *face* the things you fear.

I'm not like that, Maggie.

Because you've never tried . . .

I don't want to talk anymore.

All right, darling—go to sleep.

Lie down in darkness. Try to relax. Think of the past. Remember . . . the circus. Yes, red pink green, spangles and sawdust, cotton candy, crackerjack, elephants. How sad they are, lumbering around in a circle, each one's trunk holding another one's tail. They sit up and beg like dogs when the man prods them with a stick. They seem embarrassed. Tears come into my eyes, pity for the huge beasts who must perform like little dogs. Leo puts his arm around me. "Watch this!" A roll of drums, a flash of spotlights. Two people bow, shed their capes, and climb up and up and up. Suddenly they fall into the air like birds, back and forth, swooping. They build momentum, and the girl leaves her trapeze and soars into space alone. Oh! He has caught her at the last second, caught her hands, and the two of them swing together. Wonderful . . . but more. Acrobats and tigers. Little ponies with ribbons in their manes. A girl with red hair who rides them standing up, leaping from one to another. Sawdust filtering through spotlights. Bugles and drums. Now clowns, dozens of clowns run through the audience, and one tries to sit on my lap. Leo roars with laughter. I blush, pleased yet ashamed. Oh, it is over. So soon. But he takes me downstairs to see the animals on display. I find what I am looking for: the oldest and saddest elephant. I want to feed him, so Leo buys a bag of peanuts. The tip of the animal's trunk is soft as it snuffles up the peanuts. Can I touch him? I ask my father. "Sure. Pat his trunk." I do, and it is leathery and sad, very old. Suddenly I lean my face against the elephant and let the tears come. "Sweetheart? What's wrong?" Oh Daddy, he's so old and yet they still make him work. "No, no. You've got it all wrong. The circus is his job. He likes the circus." But he doesn't, Daddy! I can tell! Leo picks me up and holds me. "Come on, now. This fellow has a very nice life. Look how well he's kept. You think he'd ever get that fat in the jungle? Every day little boys like you feed him peanuts, and at night he sleeps on a bed of straw. Believe me, he's very happy." Maybe it's true, I think. Maybe it's really true. My father says it is, and he doesn't lie about anything. I look at the elephant again and my grief evaporates. His eyes are sad, but the mouth, perhaps, is smiling. . . . Two hours later we are eating at the kitchen table. Leo ruffles my hair and grins at Mom. "You know what this one did today, at the circus? Cried over an elephant." But his voice is strangely proud.

I woke at eleven in the morning. Maggie was at work and had left my breakfast on the table. Without thinking about it, I washed and shaved and trimmed my hair with an old pair of scissors. Then I got a summer suit out of the closet, and ironed it, and chose a tie . . . and realized that I wasn't afraid. Everything coming together for the first time . . . Maggie's words, and the past, and the hot July morning. My life. I straightened the tie, combed my hair again, and went down to the street. And all the way up on the bus I knew that I was going to be all right. Clowns and circuses, the glittering lake in the Catskills, New York pavements with mica flashing under my roller skates. Davy, it's time to come in. Supper, Davy! Meals in the kitchen. Can I stay up till ten o'clock? Please, Daddy, there's such a good movie on television. Sleep, the blue darkness, his hands tucking me in, a smell of shaving lotion and cigars. Morning. I hear his shower running and fix his coffee just the way he likes it: black with two sugars. And I lean out the window as he walks to the subway, watching him till he turns the corner. He is different from other people on the street, not just because he is mine, but because his step is lighter. The back of his head is different because he holds it straight. Sometimes he swings the briefcase. I love it when he swings the briefcase because it means he is happy, and tonight when he comes home there will be something for me in his pocket.

A Hershey bar, a bag of jelly beans. First I will hug him around the waist and then I will dive into his coat pockets, excited at the feel of the loose change, the sticks of gum, the hidden prize. . . . He is still that man, and I am still that boy—if only in memory. Tell him that. Tell him you remember.

I stepped out of the elevator and saw Ben sitting in the lounge. He put down his book, came towards me, and shook my hand. His eyes gazing into mine, no words. . . . I asked if I could go in the room, and he said yes, and I had no fear as I opened the door because I knew what I was going to do.

I did not recognize the person in the bed. He was too small to be my father, too thin. He looked like no one I had ever seen before. A tube in his arm, a plastic bottle overhead. His eyes were closed. Then I saw Mom sitting in the corner, and a nurse standing by the window . . . and realized that I was in the right room.

"Mom . . . how is he?"

Her face was blank as she glanced at me. "He had a bad night. He's resting."

"Oh. I'm sorry."

"Mrs. Williams—this is my son, David."

The nurse smiled at me, but I couldn't smile back. "He looks pretty bad."

"That's because you haven't seen him since spring." Mom's voice was cold, and the nurse must have noticed it because she said she wanted to step outside for a moment. "Do that, Mrs. Williams. You must be tired."

Then we were alone, not meeting each other's eyes. "I'm sorry I didn't come before," I said. "I've been sort of busy."

"You don't have to make excuses."

"How is he—really?"

"They have him on morphine."

"A lot of pain?"

"Yes, but he's very good about it. . . ."

Dad opened his eyes and mumbled something. "What, Leo? I didn't hear you." She walked over to him.

"I asked you what time it was."

"One-thirty."

"Is it time for my shot?"

"Not for a little while."

"I thought it was time."

"Is the pain very bad?"

"No, no, but I had a strange dream . . . a big boat."

"Leo, Davy's here."

"Really?"

I went to the bed and took his hand. It was like an old person's, dry and thin. "Dad? How are you doing?"

"Pretty good. I'll be out of here in a few weeks."

"You look fine."

"Sure, sure. Everything all right?"

"Yes," I said.

"Oh . . ."

Mom stepped between us and bent over him. "Do you want Mrs. Williams?"

"No. It's gone now."

"They'll bring the shot soon."

"I know."

"Where does it hurt? Try to tell me."

"It's nothing, just gas pains. . . . You called the office this morning?"

"Yes."

"And everything's all right?"

"The deliveries will be on schedule—don't worry about it."

"What about Mary's cold? She had a bad cold last week."

"That was long ago, Leo."

"I told her to go home, but she wouldn't. Sitting at the typewriter with this bad cold."

"She's fine, darling. You mustn't worry so much."

"Everything goes to pieces when I'm not there. . . ."

Mom glanced at me. "Davy, your father can't see you on that side."

I came around to the other side of the bed and smiled at him. "Benjamin?" he asked.

"No," I said. "It's Davy."

"Funny . . . you looked like your uncle. I was dreaming of a boat. Steerage. My father came over in steerage."

"I'm glad to see you, Dad."

"If he told the story once, he told it a million times. The crowded conditions. People got sick and one of the kids died. Ben would always get so upset by that story."

"Dad, I want to . . ."

He gazed at me. "You look so much like your uncle. . . . Can I have some water?" Mom put a straw in the water glass and lifted his head from the pillow. "Thank you."

"Don't talk," she said. "Let us do the talking."

"What's the matter? I can't visit with my own family?"

"Just try to rest."

He closed his eyes and she sat there holding his hand, her face transformed by a look I had never seen before. As though he were her child, someone small and sick who couldn't do anything for himself. She moistened her handkerchief in the glass of water and wiped his forehead. Then she watched him as he slept. He mumbled something and she said, "Shh, darling. I'm here." And I knew that I had no place in that room, or in their lives. They were far beyond me, in a world I couldn't enter, and the fact that it was my own doing didn't help me. I had come too late.

Mom didn't see me leave the room, and Ben didn't see me as I passed him in the lounge. Then I was downstairs, on the pavement, and the hot July weather hit me like a blow.

When he was well I hadn't gone. Now that he was dying I went every day. Sat in the lounge, read newspapers, drank containers of coffee. Sat there, watching the heat shimmer over the East River and listening to voices on the loudspeaker. Sat there, cold in the air conditioning, Benjamin reading in the chair across from me, my mother never leaving Dad's side. . . . Now that it was too late, I was a faithful son. And I hated myself so much that the hate spilled out of me onto other people. Onto Mom—because she was the only one Leo wanted. Onto Ben—because he seemed so tranquil with his faith in God. Onto Maggie—who tried to help me and failed. And finally onto Dad himself. Why? Because he was abandoning me. Crazy, irrational. I had abandoned *him,* and now I felt like a five-year-old being deserted. Each morning I would enter his room and stand by the bed, but he never knew me. Sometimes he called me Ben, and other times Father. He asked me to buy him a candle. He asked me to find a nickel that was lost. He said they couldn't have a *Seder* that year, and cursed a boy who had stolen Ben's jacket. He spoke of a pair of shoes and rain coming in the window . . . but he never spoke of me. I would leave the room in tears and walk the corridor. Whispered voices, nurses studying charts, trays being carried back and forth. So hot and steamy that I would gasp when I went outdoors, my hair suddenly wet, my collar soaked. Madness. I sent him flowers. And when I asked Mom if they'd arrived she looked at me without comprehension. She was like a dreamer, a sonambulist, living at the hospital yet going out once a week to have her hair done and bring clothes from the apartment. The Lowensteins came and passed me in the hall, crying. July. Thick, humid, a blackened sky out of which sheets of rain would erupt. The bus, which I took twice a day, people irritable in the heat.

One morning Leo wasn't in his room, the door open. . . . I ran to find Benjamin and learned that he had been taken to the Intensive Care Unit. So the vigil began again on the sixth floor. Intensive Care—where people went to die. Whole families standing in the hall, waiting . . . pale women with tearless eyes, mothers, sisters. Men who paced and smoked, not knowing what to do with themselves. The door of the ward swinging open to reveal masses of machinery, rows of beds. I couldn't see him and was afraid to go in, but one day I forced myself to enter that room, that place of death, and saw my father in a bed by the window. No longer human, just a thing with tubes up its nose. . . . After that I felt nothing. It rained, and I listened to the splatter of it on the windows. Ben brought me sandwiches and coffee. Then, on August third, I stepped out of the elevator and saw Mom sitting on a bench in the hall. She was staring straight ahead of her, and in her hand were Leo's eyeglasses. So I knew he had died. She didn't notice me and there was no emotion in her face. But she was holding the glasses so tightly that the veins stood out on her hand. I tried to speak to her and couldn't, and finally Benjamin came and led her away. It was many hours before she would give him the eyeglasses, and I understood that.

Preparations for the funeral . . . endless, ridiculous preparations. Which rabbi to choose, which cemetery. No room in my grandparents' plot, the grandparents I hadn't known, but a cousin was buried in Brooklyn and there was room near him, so perhaps. . . . Like a dinner party. Who will be seated next to whom. Do the dead care? I wondered. Do they really care where they are buried? Do they want to be powdered and rouged and dressed in their best clothes? Shoes on their feet and a handkerchief in the pocket? It seemed so vulgar, so dishonest, this imitation of life. . . . Maggie sat up the night before the funeral and wove a little bunch of dried flowers together. Bright colors—red, yellow, blue—and tied them with a white ribbon. I took them to the funeral parlor the next day, and they were the only thing that upset me. Not my father's death or my mother's grief, not the sadness of this world through which we pass like strangers, secret lovers of one another, not the loneliness of those who are left behind . . . but a bunch of dried flowers.

No more to write. Only ten pages left in the notebook anyway. October, and I shall start again. Return to work, salvage my life, and forget I've written this. Put it in the suitcase where I keep things I can't quite part with. My stamp collection, a rusty fountain pen, Donne's poems, a glass bird some girl gave me in grammar school. End of story.

No, there's one more thing. But I can't remember what it is. Something that happened the first time I visited Dad in the hospital, the time we argued about my clothes. Can't remember, but it seems important. Why? Something he said about. . . .

Go back.

I couldn't talk to him that day . . . he was looking at me so hungrily it turned me cold, and everything I had hoped for wasn't happening. . . . I had planned to kiss him, to make some sort of reconciliation, but none of it was possible. He asked if Maggie was feeding me properly—and that made me furious. Then he asked if our place had heat and hot water, and I felt like walking out of the room. Two years' separation, and he was right back in the old pattern: criticisms, complaints. He was dying, and knew it, yet he couldn't stop acting the boss. I could feel the tension rising between us like a tangible thing, so I changed the subject.

"Dad . . . tell me about yourself. Do you like your doctor?"

"Sure I like him. The top man in the country. He operated on one of the Kennedys."

"He must be very good then."

"You know your old man—only the best. But it worries me to see you so thin. Why don't you take a vacation? All work and no play isn't a good thing."

"Well, maybe this summer . . . ."

"You know what I was thinking before you came? Here I am, stuck in the hospital, and there's our place in Florida sitting empty. Would you like to go down for a few weeks?"

"That would be nice. I'm kind of busy, though."

"Busy! Nineteen years old and he's busy. Come to my office and you'll see what it is to be busy. I didn't get home for supper one night last week. . . . How are you fixed for money?"

"I'm making some money with my work."

"You need a little extra?"

"No."

"I read your reviews."

"What?"

"The reviews of your show. I took the subway down and got the Village papers."

"You . . . read them?"

"Sure. And I bought extra copies for the Lowensteins. Getting to be a big shot, huh? Next thing I know they'll put you in the Modern Museum."

God . . . did he really say that, or am I inventing it? No, no, he did say it . . . and I forgot. But I couldn't have forgotten something like that! It was too important. The first time he ever cared about my work. He meant it, was sincere, was . . . impressed. And I forgot it. How could. . . . Man, something has gone very wrong here because . . . because if I forgot that, what else have I forgotten? What else have I left out? Jesus, maybe nothing I've written here is accurate! Everything is crashing around in my head, and none of it makes sense. I've been sitting here for weeks, writing what I thought was the truth, and now. . . . Take a walk, think about it. No. Just go back and read your own words. From the beginning.

Dawn, and the last entry in this notebook. It should be momentous, I guess, but I just feel tired. Hundreds of pages . . . and none of them complete. As though someone else had written this. The sins of omission—isn't that what the Catholics call it? Half the story left out. *But I didn't mean to leave it out.* I wanted to see it on paper, the people we were and the people we became. I wanted to tell the truth, no matter how dreadful, so I could be free. I wanted to look at our lives in the coldest way . . . and now I have failed. Telling only half the story. My half. Showing only one person's side. I read these pages and see Leo emerge as a kind of monster, when he was only . . . what? I swear to God, I don't know. All I know is that I left things out, important things, that were connected with him. Like Mom telling me, years ago, that she married him because he was the first person who made her feel beautiful. And Ben . . . saying that he owed his book to Dad, because Dad had educated him and given him a start in life. Arnie . . . telling me that

Leo was the only man in the world he could depend on. Mr. Warner, at the office . . . "Your father is a fine man, Davy. I wouldn't work for anyone else." They saw him differently—so perhaps I never saw him at all.

The things left out . . . his love of heroes, Churchill, Eisenhower, biographies stacked beside his bed. His longing for adventure. "You know what I wanted to be when I was a kid? A test pilot. Pretty foolish, huh?" And when he bought me a piano he said he wanted to take lessons too, but felt self-conscious about it. "I'd sound like a bull in a china store . . ." And once, long ago, I gave him a book I loved called *The Family Of Man*, a beautiful book of photographs showing the sameness of people all over the world as they got born and grew up and fell in love and got old and died . . . and his face was moved as he looked at it, but he couldn't say anything. I kept waiting for a reaction, but he just nodded his head, afraid to say the wrong thing, to disappoint me. . . . Strange . . . he said he hated black people, but when Bessie got sick he went up to Harlem to see her, and paid her hospital bills, and sent her money until she could work for us again. . . . And he pretended to be tough, but when his mother died he sat in the living room and sobbed. I was five years old and I remember standing in the doorway, baffled, as Mom held him in her arms. . . .

Crazy, crazy, to live your whole life with a person and not see him. And now it's too late. I'll never know who he was. "He tries to reach you through money because money is all he has," Rick said. "He's trying to protect you from what life did to him." But I didn't listen, didn't *want* to listen. I couldn't let go of my griefs, almost as though I needed them in order to survive . . . but they kept me a child.

I can't understand all this, Leo. You spoiled me and blamed me for being spoiled. I took from you and was accused of being weak. But when I finally struck out on my own, you were threatened. You did awful things to me, hurt me so badly . . . but your father did awful things to you, and his father did the same to him. The same mistakes over and over, no one learning from the past. All those years of running . . . I ran from you only to see you everywhere, not knowing that you can't run from a thing when it's inside you. I wanted a father in my image . . . and you wanted a son in yours . . . so we missed each other at every crossroad. It's so terrible to find this out now, because I can't tell you. And even if I could, you wouldn't listen. The same old barriers would get in the way and you'd start yelling at me . . . I don't know. I can't find answers because answers are too easy. I think I've solved you, Leo, and next year I'll know that I haven't. There are only fragments of truth, little lights in the darkness. I thought I knew the truth of you when I was twelve, and I was wrong. I thought I knew the truth when I was sixteen—but it kept changing—and maybe every year of my life I'll see you differently. Maybe one person can never know another . . . just memories. Circuses and elephants. I never knew Rick, and now I love a girl who is farthest from me when she is close. But beyond the loneliness there is memory—the love I had for you when I was small and your arms were the safest place in the world. That must mean something . . . because it happened.

I keep wishing you were alive, so we could start over. I tell myself that I'd do it differently, be patient with you, try to understand . . . when I guess I'd just act the same way. There aren't many chances in life. You grow up and become what you are without realizing it. I plan to be a better person and find myself repeating all the old patterns, being selfish, not seeing people for what they are. And I don't know how to change that. . . . There are times when I feel beautiful, sexless, light, wanting nothing—but then I crash to earth again and want everything. Myself, most of all.

It's funny. I haven't got the answers, but they don't seem important anymore. The only important thing is that you lived on this earth for a while and were my father, and that I came from you, and that my children will come from me. A long line of people, blind to one another, hurting one another . . . but surviving. So that some of them can be poets, and a very few, perhaps, can change the world. And if it's true—that living is the thing, no matter how painful—then I can thank you for my life, the gift of it. . . . I don't hate you anymore, Leo. If anything, I just feel tired, the way someone feels when he has done a long day's work. I'll sleep now and dream of your sleeping, because wherever you are, I wish you peace. Maybe the soul does survive, and maybe you're in a place I can't even imagine, existing as an energy, a force, a mind mingled with stars.

My father—sleep.